The

Nevermore

First and Last

Table of Contents

CHAPTER ONE

FBI Headquarters - Philadelphia

Friday morning, March 19

"Okay, wait. I'm confused. You want to do *what*, Hank?"

"You heard me," Hank answered gruffly, and he felt rather than saw Brody stiffen next to him.

"Yeah, but...no." Stewart irritably threw down his pen, which he knew had not yet run out of ink but was still refusing to cooperate. "When I said you had a lot of input into our press release, that didn't include throwing *yourself* under the bus."

Hank shrugged. "I'm only concerned about the well-being of my party at this point. They must go on without me, and if the public thinks Dav and Rupe were involved in any of this bullshit, they'll defect in droves."

"I get it. But-"

Hank leaned forward in an almost threatening manner. "Apparently you don't, or you wouldn't be arguing with me about it."

Stewart didn't flinch and hardened his own tone in response. "In the ten years I've known you, I've *never* had to tell you not to lie. But here I am, saying exactly that twice in less than a week. There won't be a third time. The answer is no, and that's the end of it."

"For all you know, it's not a lie. I haven't even told you anything yet."

"If you truly expect me to believe that Daven forced you to turn yourself in, you're batshit crazy, Hank. I know you. And I understand why you'd want to deflect the blame from him, I really do. But you're jumping way ahead. We haven't even discussed the charges yet."

Hank stood up and began pacing around the room angrily. "The only charge that you'll ever be able to prove is blackmail. The rest is bullshit. You know that."

"No, I don't," Stewart said simply. Quietly. Almost hesitantly.

Hank turned to him with a shocked expression. "*What*?"

Stewart took a breath so deep that it hurt his lungs. "I *believe* it, but I don't *know* it. Not yet."

"Colbert does, but you don't fucking care about that," Hank retorted with a scoff.

"Mr. Bancroft," Brody said suddenly. "Please retain your calm demeanor."

Stewart nodded, keeping his eyes on Hank. "Agreed, thank you. You need to sit down and answer these items you ignored on the questionnaire, or else we can't proceed."

Hank sat back down and snatched the papers off the desk. "This phone number that I allegedly called three times around Christmas. What's it in regards to? I don't even know how to answer."

Stewart hesitated again, not wanting to fight or cause any reason for Hank to dislike him. "Look, just answer the question. Who was the number to, and why-"

"I don't *know*! Is it illegal to call phone numbers in Denver now? Why are you even suspicious about it at all? I think I deserve an explanation. No, scratch that. I absolutely, 100% deserve a goddamned explanation about why you want to know. And where is Salome, by the way?"

"Not here."

Hank bit back his retort that would have included a snotty reference to 'Captain Obvious.' "Yeah, I can see that. Is she listening to us?"

"No. As I mentioned, this conversation is being recorded, but she's not listening live. She'll hear it later. No one else is listening, either. This is you and me. Answer the question about the phone number, please."

Hank smiled sardonically and gestured with his palm up. "You first, please. I insist."

"A moment." Stewart lifted his phone receiver and dialed a number, which was obviously Salome's.

"Mr. Bancroft would like an explanation of why we're asking about the 303 number. Yeah, that one. May I tell him?" He paused, looked at Hank and shook his head slightly, then looked away again. "Thank you."

As he hung up the phone, he mouthed "sorry" so that it couldn't be heard on the recording.

"I can't tell you until after you answer the question to the best of your ability."

"No. Brody, what are my rights in regards to this matter?" He turned to look at the young man, who was bleary-eyed from being unprepared for the red-eye flight that Daven had hastily sent him on to intercept Hank.

"None that I'm aware of, sir. The question isn't out of line so far."

Hank sighed, giving up the fight at last. "The only thing I can think of was that it was Janet's cell phone number. She was delivering a document for me when she was killed. I called her once to my memory, though. Not three times, but that was three months ago. Maybe I only spoke to her once, but had to call three times to reach her? I don't know."

Stewart's heart skipped a beat as he looked down at the phone records. That would still not explain this. Then he pulled up Janet's profile again and matched it to one single call on Hank's records. He *had* called her once, he wasn't lying, but Stewart already knew that.

"You did call her once. It's right here, and it's not the same number. Any other reason you might have called it?"

"I want to know why you're asking me, or I'm not saying another word," Hank said steadily. "Brody, don't interrupt me, please. Stewart, you either tell me what this is all about, or you put me in jail now and I'll fight until the bitter end alone because I'm not putting up with this. End of story."

"Alright, alright," Stewart said wearily, rubbing his forehead and hoping the nausea would go away sooner rather than later. "We got a call from someone claiming to be her killer. About six weeks ago. He called me again last night and gave me that number, and said you called it three times, and on the right dates. He also had detailed knowledge of the crime scene that was never released. The phone was deactivated on December 26 and is untraceable, even by us."

"What the fuck," Hank muttered to himself in disbelief.

"So now," Stewart continued miserably, "you see why I'm asking. This looks bad, Hank. That's why I'm pushing you for a reasonable explanation. Anything you can tell me will be helpful."

"What kind of *detailed knowledge* did he have, exactly?"

Stewart looked like he wasn't going to answer, but he did. "That she was carrying a list of confidential information about Urbane executives. The same list that got leaked a few weeks ago. He has the copy she was carrying, he says. So...I don't really need to add anything to that, I think."

"Did you record this 'mystery' call?"

"Yes. And you will be able to listen to it after we're done with this initial deposition. Monday, most likely."

Hank shook his head for a few minutes, it was all he could do.

"Okay. So let's say she was carrying such a list, just for the fun of it. You're implying that I had her killed *before* she could drop it off to me? How does that make any sense, logistically? Why not do her in afterwards?"

"Well, our mystery caller said he thought she'd made the drop. When he realized he messed up, he ran, deactivated the number, and hasn't been in touch with you since. Went rogue on you is what he claims."

"His *claims* are utter bullshit," Hank said angrily.

"Alright," Stewart said, still trying to write something down with his misbehaving pen. Hank wordlessly handed him one of his own, then waited silently as the man took down his notes.

"Anything else to add on this issue at the moment?"

"No. I need to talk to Daven," Hank said quietly. "Will you allow me a few minutes alone?"

"You can have ten minutes. I'm going to make some more coffee." He reached over and stopped the recording device.

"Thank you." Hank turned to Brody after Stewart was gone. "You can listen if you want, but it's going to be pretty uncomfortable, not going to lie."

Brody nodded decisively. "I'll stay."

"Hank?" answered the sleepy, astonished man on the other line. "Are you alright?"

"Yeah. Dav, I'm sorry I left without telling you. Things got crazy real quick. Are you alone?"

"Yes, I'm in your guest room. The boys are still asleep. What's going on?"

Hank glanced at the clock; it was 5:15am in Los Angeles. "Jesus, sorry to wake you. I didn't even think about the time change. Hey, listen, I got your voicemail regarding your meeting this morning with your staff."

"*Our* staff, Hank."

Pause. "Right. Look, I've been thinking about it and decided I want you guys to stay completely neutral. Don't go into anything specific, or say something like you're certain I'll be found innocent, blah blah blah. It's really important that you don't take my side. Just say this is what's happened, this is what we know, now we have to wait to see what comes next. You have to be as non-committal as possible. End of story."

There was a long pause on the other line. "What *exactly* is going on, Hank?" Daven asked suspiciously.

"Nothing, yet. Haven't even met with anyone today. But whatever I do next is in your own best interests, whether you like it or not. Okay? Promise me you won't fight, and that you'll stay out-"

"Hank-"

"Don't interrupt me, please. You and Rupe *cannot* take my side. Especially you. Remember what I said about the boys."

"So this request is personal, rather than business."

"No," Hank answered hastily. "It's both. Maybe not equally, but both all the same."

Daven didn't say anything for a while, then he demanded, "I think I'm owed a better explanation than that. What are you up to?"

"Nothing!" Hank fired back. "Are you going to do as I say, or not? I need to know before I proceed here."

"Fine, so you just want me to tell everyone 'okay, nothing to see here, back to work' and think this is just going to blow over?"

"I don't want to fight with you, Dav," Hank said tiredly, returning to his normal tone. "I'm trying to protect you first, and the party second. It's extremely important that you are personally distanced from me as much as possible right now."

Daven scoffed. "I don't feel the same, Hank. It's my duty to stand up for you. As a friend, not even as an employee. It astonishes me that you're caving in and giving up just like that, and I won't accept it. I'm going to defend you, like it or not."

Hank closed his eyes and rubbed his temples. "Dav. We've known each other for too long, that's the problem right now. You're not seeing the big picture because your heart is getting in the way. Normally I would appreciate that, but not today. Use your brain, please. If you're dragged into this...if you defend me, and I go down anyway, you'll be associated with that forever. And so will the party."

"I don't care," Daven replied simply. "You're innocent. My loyalty to you is more important than this job. The party can burn down to ashes for all I care."

"You don't mean that."

"Yes, I absolutely do."

Hank knew he wasn't going to win the argument at this point unless he changed tactics drastically, and that was going to be extraordinarily painful. He dodged a wary glance at the recording device to make certain it was actually off, then inhaled deeply.

"Okay. Dav, I...maybe you shouldn't be as loyal to me as you think. I haven't been perfectly honest with you lately, and there are things that you don't know..." His voice broke a little, but he got it back together quickly. "Look, I'm not giving up.

I'm fighting this. But I'll say it one last time: distance yourself from me before it's too late. For you, and the party. But mostly for you. You need to get back to work and move on. Don't fall on your sword for me. And if I'm cleared, we'll all get back to work as usual, and no one will be worse for wear. Are we perfectly clear now?"

There was no answer from Daven, as Hank expected, and he was surprised to feel a strong burn in his eyes and tightening in his chest.

"Dav?" he prompted after a minute.

"Yes. I'll do as you say," he replied calmly. Icily.

Hank wiped his eyes. "Thanks. I'll be in touch again soon, okay? Just...stay true. Keep our good work going until I get back. Say hi to the dogs for me."

"I will."

"Alright. Goodbye for now." He hung up before Daven could say anything that would make him burst into tears, then turned to Brody.

"Maybe you shouldn't have been listening," Hank said with a humorless laugh. "You don't know me well enough to know that sometimes I have to trick Daven into doing what's best for him."

Brody was just staring at him wordlessly.

"Are you alright?" Hank asked after a moment, concerned that his young lawyer was about to bail on him. "You can go home, if you want. I don't-"

"No, sir," Brody said firmly. "I'm staying. You're right that I don't know you well, but even a stranger could tell you weren't being truthful with Daven. You haven't done anything, have you?"

"No. Well, not what they're accusing me of, anyway," admitted Hank.

Brody hesitated a little. "You still don't think Harmon is behind all this?"

"Oh he has something to do with it, but he's not the mastermind. He's not smart or devious enough. Colbert is the puppet master here; of that I have absolutely zero doubt."

Brody nodded. "They cannot legally ignore you if you accuse him outright. Formally, I mean. But without evidence it could be construed as slander, so you have to be careful."

"I'm pretty sure slander charges are the least of my worries right now."

Hank leaned back in his chair again and stared at his phone, which was still flipped open and glowing. The urge to call Dav back and smooth things out again was overwhelming. But he hit the power button and flipped it shut, then picked up the questionnaire as Stewart re-entered the room.

CHAPTER TWO

Bancroft House - early morning - Friday

"Of course he was lying, Rupert! How could you possibly think otherwise?"

"Sorry," Rupe said contritely. "I didn't mean to imply…look, I'm just having a hard time absorbing this whole thing. Not to mention I'm still half-asleep. We've been through this before, you know. It's like freakin' Groundhog Day."

"What? I don't understand that reference."

Rupe was a little shocked at that. "You haven't seen the movie? Never mind. I mean this whole doubting him back-and-forth between you and me. Doesn't this happen every few months? Usually I'm the one being the devil's advocate because we have to look at this fairly, but that doesn't mean I'm accusing him of anything. We *know* he's done stupid, shady things in the past, Dav. This isn't-"

"No. If you're not going to get on the same page with me, just forget ever discussing this again."

Rupert sighed. "Fine. This linear thinking isn't constructive, just so you know. But if Hank wants us to distance ourselves, we have to do it. He's still the boss as far as I'm concerned. No offense, of course."

Daven stared at the ceiling fan as it slowly made its way around in endless, meaningless circles. *Kind of like this investigation, and my relationship with Rupert, and politics in general…*

"I can't do it, Rupe. I just can't sit by and say nothing in his defense. I'm going to quit."

"Right, because that solves everything, huh? Coward's way out, if you ask me."

Sigh. "I know. You're right. But it's tempting, all the same."

There was a knock on Daven's door, and he sat up so fast it made him dizzy. Shannon leaped off the bed like a flying squirrel and immediately launched into a frenzied barking fit at the door.

"Shannon, shush. Hang on, Rupe. Going to put you on mute for a moment. *Shannon* !" He climbed out of bed and went to open the door, where Theo was standing there expectantly.

"Everything okay, Theo?"

"Chef wants to know what you want for breakfast."

"Already?" Dav exclaimed as he looked at his watch.

"We eat at 7, Uncle Dav. Are you hungry yet?"

"Yes, just tell him to make whatever he's making you two. Thanks. Listen, I'm on a call and I have to finish it up. I'll be out soon."

Theo's eyes widened. "With dad?"

Daven's heart dropped a little. "Uh, no. But it's about your dad, and it's really important. I'll see you at 7, okay? Please take Shannon out and let her into the yard."

Theo frowned and took her collar wordlessly, leaving Daven feeling sorry for speaking more harshly than he intended. Hank's remarks about his rusty people skills came flooding back to him. He would have to work on that, for sure. But not right now.

"Rupe, I don't even know what to say at the staff meeting. This has really thrown me for a loop."

"Okay, let me think about it and get back to you. Try to stay focused and don't let the boys see you rattled. By the way...you know I don't like to disagree with you, but Hank's right. We have to stay neutral, and that would apply for anyone in the same situation. To do otherwise could backfire on us to the point where we can't recover."

"Honestly, I wouldn't even care."

"Daven ," Rupert admonished. "You're not acting anything like the leader Hank wants you to be. We have 509 people directly counting on us. Do you think he'd be proud of you if he heard this conversation? Proud that you gave up within five minutes and were willing to throw everything away to do the opposite of what he's asking you to do?"

"No," Daven admitted grudgingly. "He'd tear me a new one."

"Correct, and you'd deserve it. So get yourself together, and let's meet at the office at 8:30."

"Alright. Thanks. See you then."

Daven hung up and then made his way upstairs to Floyd's room in order to keep himself occupied enough to not have to think about this whole sorry situation. He was surprised to see all three dogs in bed with the teenager, wrapped around his body protectively.

"Hey, Floyd," he said softly as he approached the bed. "Time to get ready for breakfast. Are you awake?"

"I don't want to, Uncle Dav."

"Okay. You don't have to eat, but you need to go to school."

"I know," came the muffled reply. "I will."

Dav weighed the option of admonishing him about the dogs, but didn't see any benefit to being a hardass about it. Floyd was clearly comforted by their presence, and the three pairs of dark canine eyes were watching Dav so smugly that it seemed fruitless to challenge their cozy stronghold. Instead, he left and stood in the doorway of Theo's room.

"Floyd doesn't want to eat. Can you tell Chef when you go down?"

Theo was sorting through several shirts in an effort to decide what to wear. "But he always says that, and then he changes his mind at the last second. All it takes is some bacon."

"Good to know. Why didn't you take Shannon outside like I asked you?"

"She didn't want to go. It's like she suddenly weighs 500 pounds when you try to get her to do something she doesn't want to."

"Fair enough." That was indeed quintessentially Shannon, the most determined and stubborn dog he'd ever known. "But how did she and the other dogs get upstairs, then?"

Theo shrugged. "I opened the gate to let them all come up. Dad's not here."

This was an argument for another time, Daven knew instinctively, but he couldn't just let it go. "Your dad's rules still apply, Theo. Next time don't do that, or at least ask me."

"Or what? You'll take a belt to me?" Theo responded bitterly, still not making eye contact. "It's a stupid rule."

Oh boy, thought Daven. *Danger zone.* He walked fully into the room and shut the door behind him, then sat down on Theo's bed next to the pile of shirts.

"I don't believe in corporal punishment, as you know. Stop what you're doing for a second and look at me," he commanded gently, but firmly. "Thank you. I'm really disappointed in you, Theo. I've been here all of one day - less than one day, actually - and already you're testing me. We will follow *all* of your dad's rules...yes, I include myself in that, because there are plenty of things I can't do, either. It's what he wants and expects us from us. Let's not let him down. Are we agreed?"

"But it's not like he'll ever find out, since he's not coming back."

Daven closed his eyes briefly, silently vowing that he wouldn't let his sudden surge of strong emotion take over. "Go put the dogs in the yard, and don't argue with me."

Theo's posture relaxed, the fight in him disappearing instantly. "But I'm not trying to argue," he said quietly, his voice trembling a little. "Dad always lets Floyd sleep on the couch with them on bad days and it helps a lot. I was just trying to make him feel better. Sorry, Uncle Dav."

Daven froze, then before he could stop himself, he capitulated. "Okay. They can come upstairs from now on."

Theo stared agape a time him. "Really?"

"Yes. I don't want Floyd sleeping downstairs at night. So you boys will have to make sure the doors are always closed to the other rooms so they don't destroy anything."

That cheered Theo up beyond compare, but the now severely depressed Daven went back to the guest room in defeat. When he emerged forty-five minutes later the dogs were outside and Floyd was hovering over the bacon, just as Theo had predicted. *Thank god.* Floyd *was* visibly better, if not downright cheerful, but Dav knew Hank would ream him anyway when he found out.

But...maybe he didn't have to tell him. Just this once.

Denver, same time

Lester Boyd hadn't seen Harmon in many years, not since he'd left Colorado and headed for warmer climate. They had been good friends, and Harmon gave him a job for life at a party-affiliated training school, but his involvement with the party itself was long over. That's why he was still in a bit of a daze as he waited in the conference room for his old friend, but he was smart enough to realize that this undoubtedly had something to do with Hank Bancroft. But what, he didn't know and couldn't fathom.

Colbert, though…he was another story altogether. Lester and Colbert hadn't been on speaking terms since pretty much their first meeting. He couldn't understand what Harmon saw in the quietly dangerous man who locked eyes with people during conversation like his life depended on it. It was unnerving and intimidating, exactly what was intended. That was why Lester stiffened when he heard the distinctive voice just outside the door. The knob turned along with his stomach.

"Lester Boyd," Colbert sing-songed as he entered the room with Harmon. "Long time, no talk. You look old, my friend."

"Thank you?"

Harmon silently shook hands with him, but Colbert just sat down and spread papers in front of himself as cheerfully as if they were all about to play dominoes.

"Thanks for coming," Harmon said guardedly. "You must be incredibly curious why I asked you here, and I'll explain. I'll also compensate you for the time you had to take off from work. But first I want to ask you something. Are you following the news in regards to Hank Bancroft?"

Lester cleared his throat and sat up straighter. "Only out of morbid curiosity, really. Those media idiots don't really know what's going on and their theories change every five minutes."

"Right. Well, as you know, I'm not a fan of Hank's personality and tactics. We've fought a lot over the years, and only recently started getting along and working together on some measures."

"So I've heard," Lester said with a grin. "Nobody thought you and Hank could agree on the color of an orange."

Harmon didn't smile back. "You're not wrong. But one thing we have always agreed on is how we would do anything to protect our children. Hank is facing prison time, and the reason behind it is highly confidential. I've been tasked with finding a mutually agreeable negotiator, which is why I asked you here."

"You mean...to negotiate what's going to happen to Floyd and Theo?"

"Yes. I know you two aren't exactly friends, but you spent six years with the boys and ten years with Hank. Do you think he'd be willing to speak to you on my behalf regarding the plea bargain? If you agree, I can tell you everything. Then you'll have to meet with him and discuss terms. He's a good father, he'll do what's best for his boys."

A good father. He wondered how Harmon knew that, and felt a cold surge of nostalgia at the sudden recollection of what Hank's parenting was like back in the days just after the revolution. To a casual observer, he'd actually been a terrible father to the boys, especially to Floyd - controlling, harsh, and downright unreasonable the majority of the time. Lester had often stepped in to comfort young Floyd after a punishment. But Hank wasn't what he seemed; he spent half the time struggling to protect them, and half the time spoiling them senseless, which was what he vastly preferred.

Good father or not, he deeply loved his sons. If they were threatened in any way, no force in the universe could survive the wrath he would unleash on the culprits. Lester had seen it with his own eyes. They were threatened now, and Hank must be out of his mind with worry.

Lester cleared his throat again, and then took the bottle of water that Harmon hastily pushed over to him. "Thanks," he said after he drank half of it. "I said I'd kill Hank the next time he saw me. So I would say my chances of getting any conversation out of him would be 50-50. Useful conversation, on the other hand…maybe a 10% chance. There's just one problem beyond my ability to solve, though."

"What's that?"

"He'll never bargain. Not with you, with me, with anyone. Never has, never will. He'll go down swinging first, and damn the consequences."

Harmon knew this, of course. "Let's just get to the end result that I'm hoping for: as the aggrieved party Hank's sons can be deeded to me via the plea bargain. I'll transfer them to Daven myself after the trial, if he makes it through."

"Makes it through?"

"Yes. I learned yesterday that Daven is also implicated in at least one of the charges the FBI is bringing against Hank. A minor one, but enough to potentially earn him a class 2 felony and put him out of the running as their guardian."

Oh…fuck. Lester almost choked, but he managed to keep a straight face. "Okay. But deeds can only be transferred once a year. Hank will never agree to you having them for a year, or a day, and that's if he even believes you'd actually do it. Not in a million years, with a million words and a million promises."

"I know, but we have to try. Didn't say this job was going to be easy. And I can't compensate you for it, either. We have to move fast if you're going to agree, though. I'll need you in Philadelphia on Tuesday at the latest."

"Move fast?" Lester asked. "Why rush it? Something like this...you'll need all the resources and time you can get."

Harmon glanced aside at Colbert; Lester really *was* out of the loop now on the world around him now that he'd all but left the party.

"I think we're going to need more time than I allotted for this discussion." He stood up. "Let me go clear my calendar."

Seditionist HQ, 10am staff meeting

Daven felt all but paralyzed as he stood in the wings at the little basement theater that was housed in the office park. Rupert had hastily rented the venue from the owner of the building for an exorbitant fee, and all 488 employees present were jammed in shoulder to shoulder, waiting eagerly for news from their executives. He prayed no one would think to call the fire department and report a violation; the last thing the Seditionists needed right now was more bad PR over jamming their entire staff into a fire trap.

"Dav," Rupert said gently, moving closer towards his new boss. "It's 10. You got to go out and talk to them. Come on."

"I...Rupe, I've never been so nervous in my life."

"I don't envy you, but you have to do it. Go get it over with."

Daven took a deep breath. "Alright. Where's the mic, Taylor?"

Taylor glided over and handed it to him, then put a finger over her lips and turned on the switch. The light on the bottom of the mic glowed green and squealed briefly; Rupert imagined feeling his own heart squeal back in response as he handed over the little speech they'd written together. He felt damnably sorry for Dav, but this was his job now and he had to do it. Hank had been through much worse a dozen times over.

Daven closed his eyes, prayed silently for what seemed like an interminably long time, and walked out onto the little stage without any further adieu.

"Good morning," he said first, and everyone murmured the same back in response. Dav froze; not because of stage fright but because he was afraid that his tone of voice would lack the conviction and strength he needed to get through this. It was hard enough to convince people of something you believed in, and much harder to convince them of something you didn't. He looked down at the paper and realized his hands were shaking; which oddly helped steady his nerves. *Let my hands shake, then...as long as my voice doesn't.*

"We're under a media gag order right now, so this message is for your ears only. We will make a public statement on Monday." Deep breath. "Hank Bancroft has been taken into custody pending charges that could lead to a criminal conviction. While the investigation is ongoing, I will be the interim leader of the Seditionists.”

He stopped, folded up the paper and put it in his pocket, imagining Rupert all but screaming from him from the wings for going off-script after just two sentences. *How often have we both done the same to Hank?* he wondered briefly, sadly.

“Hank wishes for me to not defend him, to not say he’s innocent, to not...put myself in a position where it could backfire and give me a bad name if the worst happens. I fought him hard on that, but ultimately agreed that it was in the best interests of our party - of all of *you* - that we allow him to independently proceed through this investigation, no matter what any of us personally believes. But I’ve worked for Hank for 10 years and been friends with him for 12, so you can probably imagine exactly how I feel about this entire situation. Which is that the accusations are complete bullshit, by the way, in case you have any doubts. But again, Hank told me not to say that, so I won’t.”

“Jesus Christ,” whispered Rupe to Taylor in shock. “Dav has gone rogue. Never thought I’d see the day.”

“I knew he had it in him,” Taylor responded with a smirk.

Daven stopped to take a deep breath and then walked up to the very edge of the stage, taking a moment to try to look at every face in the room. “Just because I’m up here on stage five feet above you does not mean I consider any of you below me. *All* of us have *equal* responsibility to honor Hank’s legacy by respecting his wishes to continue our good work in his absence, and to not waste time and words speculating about what could be. Therefore, at this time I will make no further remarks on the situation, because I don't have time for it. It's back to business for all of us. We have an April 1 vote coming up, and several of the measures still need a lot of work as far as rallying our constituents to oppose them. I would encourage you to avoid the news for now since we don't need the distraction of mindless media speculation. As I mentioned, our media statement will be released on Monday. Thank you for your cooperation."

He walked offstage and handed the mic back to Taylor, then looked at Rupe as he loosened his tie, expression as guilty as a dog who had been caught raiding the trash.

"Go ahead," he said with a resigned sigh. "Chew me out for not following the script."

"You think I should?" Rupert answered seriously.

"If I was Hank, you would."

"You're not Hank. He usually went off-script to spite me. You did it to honor him. I'm actually *really* proud of you, Dav." Rupe's voice cracked a little, and even he seemed surprised at himself for saying it.

Daven froze with his tie half off. "Wait. What?"

Rupert clapped him on the shoulder, feeling a warm glow course through both of them. "You did good. Really good. Hank would hate it, but I loved it. It was what our team needed to hear. Just don't give that same speech to the cameras on Monday, please, or I might have something vastly different to say about it."

"I won't. Is it too early to go get lunch?"

"Not really. Blue Daisy opens at 10:30. Want to walk over?"

"Yes, please. I need a drink."

CHAPTER THREE

FBI HQ - Philadelphia

Four hours into the interview, when it was time to break for the afternoon, Stewart was all but at the end of his rope with Hank's answers. Not that there was anything wrong with them, but...ironically enough, come to think of it, the problem was *exactly* that there was nothing wrong with them. No conclusions could be drawn, no coincidences struck away, no questions answered...nothing. They ended the morning where they had started it, and the only thing gained was a new level of frustration and distrust from both sides.

The next hour or so was going to be much harder. Exponentially harder. Stewart had to introduce the idea of a negotiator, which he knew Hank would absolutely throw a shit fit about. Then, as the day ended, he would have to call Harmon and inform him that Janet might have been carrying the list of confidential information for Hank. He wasn't looking forward to either task, to say the least, so he just sat there alone, forcing down the tasteless whatever-was-on-his-plate, wondering what the hell Hank was thinking right now.

He sure knew what his own thoughts were like, and they're weren't pretty.

Hank roamed around the room restlessly while Brody hungrily ate another snack, and wondered what the hell Stewart was thinking about. It took a tremendous amount of willpower to fight the temptation to call his sons. They were in school, he knew, and what exactly was he going to tell them anyway? What was he going to tell Daven, for that matter? Or anyone? He knew he was screwed on just the blackmail charge alone; the rest of it almost didn't matter at this point.

Then there was Harmon. How tempting it was to call him, too. Stewart never explained what he meant when he'd said Harmon was on Hank's side, and the real translation of what that meant was an agonizing itch that Hank couldn't scratch. He resolved to ask the question directly, and then automatically pulled his phone out of his pocket to call Daven.

Los Angeles

"Hello Hank," Dav answered gruffly. "I have Rupert with me. Is it ok if I put you on speaker?"

"Sure."

Rupert took a deep breath and sat down in Daven's desk chair, ignoring the astonished side-eye he was getting from his new boss.

"It's weird not having you here, Hank," Rupe said matter-of-factly. "Can't wait for you to get back and start bitching about Daven's caffeine intake again."

"You mean the fact that he goes through an entire package of my espresso pods every day? I don't miss that. Damned things are expensive. Hey...did a guy come in to seal up my office door?”

“Yes,” Daven answered quickly, then he covered the phone’s microphone with his hand. “Out of my chair,” he hissed in irritation at his colleague.

“I can imagine what everyone must be saying,” continued Hank glumly, his voice tinny and far away over the flip phone. “Don’t tell me, it will just make me more depressed.”

Rupert answered in a positive tone, although his body language was saying something else to Daven entirely. “I would love to tell you what they’re saying, actually. It would raise your spirits quite a bit.”

“Hmmm. Speaking of which, Dav, how did the meeting go this morning?”

“It wasn’t a meeting,” Daven said as he sat down in his reclaimed chair, while Rupert took the couch off to the side. “I...I just had some things to say.”

“Did you distance yourself from me like you promised?”

Dav shot a warning look at Rupert before responding. “Hank, I made it clear that we as an organization were to let you proceed through the investigation independently and without offering any opinions to the contr-”

“Just answer the question, Dav,” Hank interrupted tiredly. “I wanted you to not back me up and stay entirely neutral. Did you, or did you not do specifically that?”

The long silence that ensued answered the question for them all.

"Right," Hank sighed, sounding rightfully disappointed. "Maybe you should take me off speaker for a moment. I want to say something to you privately."

Daven picked up the phone and took a deep breath as he hit the button. "Yes? It's just me now."

"Look, Dav. I know I'm not in charge of you right now, but-"

"You are, Hank. Until this ends, one way or another."

Pause. "If you really believe that, you wouldn't have disobeyed me. *Again.* Tell me exactly what you said."

Daven hesitated. "I'd rather not, because you might have a stroke."

"That might be a blessing in disguise. Tell me."

Dav did, almost word for word.

"Okay," Hank eventually responded. "Obviously it's no surprise that I'm really pissed off with you right now, and it frustrates me to the extreme that you can't understand why. If my boys really don't matter to you that much, then I might as well just turn them over to the state right now and save us all the trouble. Because I'm going down, Dav, whether you want to believe it or not. It's time to get some fucking common sense, accept the reality of this situation, and start thinking about someone other than yourself. Are you hearing me?" His tone and volume had escalated dramatically, shocking Daven to the core. It took him a few moments to find his voice.

"I'm not going to apologize for supporting you, Hank. I never will, no matter how angry you get."

Hank scoffed angrily. "Fine. Tell that to the boys when you're not approved to be their guardian after this shitshow goes through the courts. I'm sure they'll understand that you couldn't set your pride aside for five minutes to save them 20 years of slavery."

"It's not pride. It's loyalty."

"I don't give a shit what it is, you're endangering my sons and I don't appreciate it one bit. Put Rupert back on the phone."

Dav shakily hit the speaker button once again. "Okay. He's back on."

"Rupe?"

"Yes, Hank?" he answered in a timid voice while watching Daven worriedly; the man had suddenly gone ashen and looked about to vomit.

"I'm going to give it to you straight. If Dav doesn't toe the line, he's going to get dragged into this mess even further, which means Floyd and Theo are in serious trouble. The Seditionists are to stay neutral and not defend me, period. I said it before and I'll say it until my dying breath. Do you understand why?"

"Yes, sir, completely understood." Rupert never called Hank *sir* unless he was dead serious and totally sincere...which wasn't very often at all. Therefore, Hank knew for certain that his friend needed no further explanation and would do as asked without question.

"Thank you," he breathed in relief. "Daven? What about you? Are you going to comply with my wishes now?"

"Yes, sir." It was even more rare for Daven to use the honorific, and Hank was satisfied at last.

"Good," he responded happily, tone back to normal again. "Then get back to work. The April 1 vote is coming up, and Harmon wants to work with you on it. I expect you to cooperate fully with him despite this entire sorry situation, because our constituents are more important than personal grudges. I'll be in touch soon."

Daven said nothing more as Rupert bid their boss farewell and ended the call almost as pleasantly as it had begun.

"Jesus, Dav," Rupe breathed shakily as he closed the phone and handed it back to his friend. "I never realized how scary he can be over the phone. In person, yes, but this is new. We'd better do what he says. Are you...are you alright? You're white as a sheet."

"I'm fine," Daven snapped as he got up to get some coffee. Then, remembering what Hank had said about the espresso pods, he stopped and resolved to curb his caffeine habit. Maybe that would ease his temper somewhat.

"Sorry, Rupert," he finally said. "I'm not myself today, obviously. I'm going to call Hank back and apologize. Do you mind..."

"Not at all, leaving now. Lock your door so you don't get interrupted."

"Thanks. I haven't forgotten about our lunch. Just give me a few minutes."

"Sure."

Daven got up and made the espresso anyway, swiftly abandoning his plan to cut back in favor of a quick fix of energy. Then he sat down in front of his desk phone and stared at it gloomily, unmoving.

After twenty minutes he still hadn't dialed the phone. He didn't want to. He knew he unfairly pointed the finger at Hank for this entire situation, for thrusting him prematurely into this job as CEO and father figure. Positions he *didn't want*, he realized with a jolt for the very first time.

Even as the ugly truth set in, he hoped and prayed he would come around and actually want these things. Sooner, rather than later.

If he'd had the *choice* to take them, would he want them then? Was his reticence only because the boys and this job were forced on him? Was he being completely unreasonable and childish?

He didn't know. It was possible. All that was for certain right now was the fact that forgiveness and understanding weren't his number one priorities at this time. Saving his friend *was*, but he wasn't being allowed to even attempt it; his way blocked by the very man who needed saving.

It was such a fucked up situation, and to put it plainly...Daven blamed Hank entirely and resented him bitterly for it. Even as he fought not to, and knew it was wrong.

But he also knew sitting around and moping was accomplishing nothing, so he shoved the phone angrily away and got up to collect Rupert for lunch at Hank's favorite restaurant.

Had Daven known that he would never have the opportunity to speak to Hank again, the morning would have ended quite differently.

CHAPTER FOUR

Friday night - Los Angeles

It was suppertime at the Bancroft house, and Floyd and Theo waited politely and silently at the table while Chef kept the food heated for them. Normally, Chef would be home in Eagle Rock with his family on a Friday night but Daven didn't know that, and had earlier in the day asked him to prepare a nice meal for dinner. Vance had taken pity on the man and promised to drive him personally home afterwards, an offer which Chef had gratefully accepted.

The servants all instinctively knew tough times were ahead, even though - like Floyd and Theo - they were not allowed to watch live television in the house. They could watch movies and TV series on tapes that Maurice would rent from Blockbuster on a weekly basis, but that was it. It was a rule universally resented by all of the indentured staff, but considering the lengths to which the man ensured their comfort and happiness in other ways - some quite extraordinary, such as the weekly banquets with their families - no one ever dared to complain, nor to even think of complaining. It almost seemed treasonous to even grumble about such a minor thing.

Maurice was also here, but that was normal since he lived in the house full time. At the moment he was busily canceling all the arrangements for the planned weekend sailing trip and Disneyland, taking some comfort in the fact that neither of the boys had known about the outings before Hank had left for

Philadelphia. He couldn't imagine either one of them even wanting to go anyway, considering the circumstances...well, maybe Theo would. He was too young to be perturbed by much, thankfully.

At a quarter after seven, Floyd got up from the table and told Theo he was cold and going to get a sweater. Instead, he snuck downstairs to Brittany's office. She was there, watching the news and drinking tea with an absent-minded expression.

"Hey Floyd," she said warmly. The next words out of her mouth should have been, "you aren't allowed down here," but the truth was, she didn't care. The poor kid had been through enough lately and didn't need his guards hounding him.

"Hi." Floyd looked up at the television, then back to Brittany. "Do you think dad's coming back?" he asked quietly.

Brittany frowned, then set her cup down carefully. "He hasn't told me what's going on. But I've heard from Avery that it's...that it's possible Hank, I mean, your dad, might have to stay away for awhile." She glanced at the news footage. "The news is even less helpful than Avery was, no big shocker there," she said skeptically.

Floyd sat down on the corner of her desk and began to watch the news, pointedly crossing his arms to show that he didn't care about the rule saying he couldn't. But the screen went black suddenly, and he turned to look at Brittany. His words of protest died on his lips; she was holding the remote with a resolute and business-like expression, finger still on the power button.

"We can talk all you want, but I'm not turning it back on."

"Just for a minute?" Floyd pleaded.

"Nope. I'd like to keep my job, Floyd. I really like being here with you and your brother."

"Okay. Sorry." Floyd shrugged and went back upstairs. He bypassed the first floor and went straight to Hank's sitting room, punching in 1182 in the entry panel, marveling at how easy it was to figure out the code. His dad used Theo's birthday for pretty much everything.

He parked himself on the couch and turned on the TV, feeling his stomach turn at the sight of Hailey Hendricks reporting from a driveway. *His* driveway, actually. Of course.

Before I send it back to you guys in the studio, I wanted to stress that the media statement distributed only an hour ago made it clear that the party is taking a huge step back from Mr. Bancroft, by outright refusing to defend him or even take his side. It almost seems like - and you might have to kind of read between the lines for this one - that Mr. Johansson is perhaps even responsible for the quick exit to Philadelphia. One can imagine that he is deeply concerned about his own role in all of this, probably even afraid of how it will impact his career, and is taking steps to mitigate the damage as much as possible.

What do you mean by responsible, Hailey? asked a weasley-looking studio anchor as the camera flashed to him. *Surely you don't mean Daven Johansson is responsible for Hank's arrest?*

Hailey smiled in a sinister fashion that made Floyd's skin crawl. *It's possible when you think about why he would*

Floyd leaped to his feet and slammed his hand down hard on
the power button of the television, almost knocking the screen
over in the process. He couldn't breathe, and his hands were
numb, not feeling the stairwell railing at all as he raced back
down the stairs. The wall rumbled next to him on the landing,
indicating the massive garage door opening or closing. Either
way, that meant Uncle Dav had arrived at last.

Floyd veered into his room, locked the door behind him, and
dived under the covers, laying perfectly still as Hailey's shrill
accusations repeated in his brain over and over again. Less
than two minutes later his heart stopped when he heard Daven

Johansson - the *next leader of the Seditionists* - knock on the door to his room. Floyd pulled out his cell phone and called his dad as fast as his shaking fingers could manage.

Two times. Three times.

There was no answer.

The door to the room jiggled a little, then opened wide. Floyd pulled the blanket tighter over his head and held his breath.

Friday night, Philadelphia

Hank laid back down in his hotel's bed and seethed freely for the third hour in a row. He was still beyond appalled at Harmon's offer of a negotiator, and had nearly physically assaulted Stewart just for mentioning it. Fortunately he kept his wits about him, and carried on the conversation to the bitter end...during which he had somehow agreed to the negotiator - on his own accord, not coerced - and he was pissed as hell about it. But he knew Stewart was trying to help, and that was the only saving grace in this situation.

What was worst of all was that his phone had been taken away from him after Harmon quickly reported to Stewart that Hank had called him. It was true; Hank had given in to his curiosity immediately after the tough conversation with Daven. Rather than submit to charges of contempt and go straight to jail, he agreed to give up the phone in exchange for maintaining his freedom...well, what limited amount of freedom he had, anyway. His hotel room's phone was taken out, and a guard stationed outside to prevent him from leaving. But as pissed off as he was about the situation, he knew it was better than jail and therefore resolved to make the best of it. Stewart had promised to give him back the phone the next morning at 10am, and warned that any further attempts would result in a felony contempt charge.

So now there was nothing to do but seethe, order room service, and sleep. Hank did plenty of the first one, and even more of the second just out of spite (until he got cut off by the irritated guard), and exactly none of the third. It was a very long night for the soon-to-be former leader of the Seditionists.

Los Angeles

"Floyd?" asked Daven gently, not stepping into the bedroom just yet.

"Mmmph?"

"Uh...dinner is ready. What are you doing?"

Floyd mumbled that he was cold, and Daven waited a few long moments and then walked up to the bed, keeping a respectful distance.

"Come down and eat. The food will warm you up."

"I want to talk to dad."

"I do too, Floydie. We can't until tomorrow. Come down and eat."

"My name is Floyd," he replied sharply.

"Okay, *Floyd* . In a bit of a temper, I see. Shall I have chef bring up a plate for you?"

Floyd turned around and peered at the man he suddenly could feel no warmth for. "Chef is supposed to be in Eagle Rock."

Daven cocked his head. "What do you mean?"

Floyd turned back around and faced the wall, saying nothing. Let him flounder and figure it out for himself.

Daven didn't take the bait; he knew exactly what Floyd was doing. "Alright, I'll ask Theo. I know why you're upset, and you're right. I should have called. The day got away with me. I didn't mean to get home so late. Will you come down to dinner?"

"This isn't your *home* ," Floyd blurted hotly. "It's mine and Theo's, and it belongs to our *dad* . Remember him?"

Floyd didn't even care that Daven's expression was at once crestfallen and stunned and hurt. He set his jaw even tighter, resolving to say nothing further.

Dav responded in a strangled tone. "Alright, Floyd, we're going to nip this in the bud right now. Let's have a talk."

Floyd threw his covers off and sat up abruptly. He absolutely hated the *let's have a talk* spiel; it didn't matter who said it, or for what reason - good or bad. "Theo's waiting for us," he grumbled irritably.

"He can wait a minute or two longer." Daven sat down on Floyd's desk chair. "Truthfully, Floyd, I trip over saying the word *home* every time I say it when it's not referring to my house down the street. It's really awkward, but I mean well. What would you prefer me to say instead?"

That threw Floyd off completely; he had been spooling up for a fight and was now being asked for advice instead?

"Say *the house* ," he finally mumbled.

"Deal. Now, if there's something bothering you besides that, and besides the obvious fact that you're missing your dad, please tell me. I believe open communication is the key to preventing and solving all problems."

Floyd took the ball and ran with it. "Fine. I heard the party was going to release a media statement today in regards to my dad. What did it say?"

Daven didn't hesitate; he reached into his pocket and pulled out a paper that had a few typed sentences on it and all kinds of handwritten notes.

"This is what you're getting all bent out of shape for? Why didn't you just ask me to begin with?"

"Can I read it?"

"Sure."

Floyd took it as if it were on fire and read it carefully.

Daven Johansson, interim leader of The Seditionists, is obliged to issue a blanket "no-comment" statement for the duration of the trial of Hank Bancroft. Party business will continue as normal, effective immediately. A press conference to discuss the April 1 voting docket will be held on March 25 at 10am PST. This will be followed by twenty minutes of Q&A,

Floyd read it three times, then looked up with a carefully blank
expression. "What does the *topical* thing mean?"

"It means that questions not relating directly to the April 1
vote will be ignored because they're not the point of the press
conference."

Meaning questions about his dad. Floyd was feeling hot again.
"You didn't defend dad at all. Why?"

Daven took the paper back and folded it up, slipping it back
into his pocket for safekeeping. He was only slightly mollified
to realize Floyd hated it as much as he did. That it hurt his own
heart as much as it hurt Floyd's, even if it was just a statement
aimed directly at the media and not at his own constituents.
That would come later and it would be much harder to craft,
even with Hank's guidance.

"It's complicated, Floyd," he finally said, reluctantly. "I
wouldn't even know how to explain."

Floyd's heart suddenly flushed ice cold at that. So it was
exactly as Hailey had said, after all. Daven was distancing
himself from his dad in order to protect himself. Abandoning
him. Possibly he had even been the one to... *no* .

"I'm not hungry, Uncle Dav." *Uncle Dav.* The words sounded
traitorous on his dry tongue. "You should get down to Theo or
he's going to start pouting. I'm going to bed."

"Alright. You know where the refrigerator is if you change your mind." Daven stood up and went to the door. "Goodnight, Floydie."

"Floyd."

"That's right, sorry. Goodnight, Floyd."

Daven waited for a response and got nothing.

Floyd waited for the door to shut, then got out his phone again and dialed his dad in vain for almost two hours.

CHAPTER FIVE

Saturday morning - Philadelphia

Hank Bancroft finally did fall asleep, but it wasn't until 9am. He was awakened at 10 by Stewart, who wished to return his cell phone as promised.

"Morning, sorry to wake you." Stewart set the phone down on the credenza - after thoughtfully plugging it into the charger he had also taken away - and started to back out of the hotel room again. "It goes without saying that we'll be monitoring your calls, so…"

"Yeah, I know. Hey, what's on the agenda for today? For me, I mean."

"Nothing, actually. You're confined to the hotel grounds, of course, which shouldn't be too much of a hardship."

Hank smiled a little. "Yeah. I'm sure the public would love to hear how their tax dollars are going towards putting a disgraced criminal up in a five-star hotel for a week."

"That's *not* what you are, and besides, they're not paying for it. It'll be billed to the Seditionists, of course."

Hank recalled all the ridiculously expensive room service he had ordered last night and grimaced hard. So much for sticking it to the man. "Oh. Well, then…you couldn't have put me up at the Hilton again or something?"

Now it was Stewart's turn to grin. "You'll have to take that one up with your chief of staff. I was going to put you there, but Daven threw a fit and insisted on this."

Of course , Hank groaned internally. "Right. I'll be sure to knock another star off his chart, then."

Stewart nodded, then got serious again as he pointed back at the phone. "I know it's totally none of my business, but you have quite a few missed calls from your son. About 40 or so. I had to turn the vibration alerts off, it was driving me nuts."

"I'm sure. Thanks. So when do I have the pleasure of the FBI's company again?"

"Tomorrow morning. Do you want to go to church?"

"No."

"Okay. I'll be here to pick you up at nine. We'll spend most of the day going over your deposition and making any corrections or clarifications. Monday will be your day to decide where you want to go next, and the negotiator will arrive on Tuesday."

Hank swallowed hard. "Do you know who it is?"

"Yes, but I can't tell you. I'm sorry." Stewart blushed as he vaguely waved around the room. "You should, uh...try to get as much rest as possible today. I apologize for interrupting your sleep."

"Mmhmm. Thanks." Hank was secretly amused by the fact that Stewart was apparently just *now* finding it awkward to be holding such a serious conversation with one of them half-naked in bed.

"Okay. See you tomorrow."

"Wait," Hank said quickly, "Is my guard at this hotel, also?"

"Yes, Avery is next door, room 1147. I know you prefer connecting rooms, but under the circumstances-"

"I know. Don't worry about it. Thanks."

Stewart left, and Hank laid back and stared at the ceiling for a long time until he remembered the remark about all of Floyd's missed calls. He waited a few more minutes, then dragged himself into the shower to clear his mind and think about what he was going to say to his kids.

Los Angeles - Saturday morning

Daven hadn't slept all night, either. He was too busy actively hating everything and everybody, and turning over a thousand different scenarios in his mind - almost all of them dire and bleak. It was almost 8am, and he was no longer able to resist the urge to call Hank. 11am in Philadelphia; surely the man was awake by now even though he was well-known for his ability to sleep far past the noon hour.

So he picked up his phone and dialed, still somehow not surprised to find himself listening a few rings later to Hank's voicemail message. Still asleep, then. He dialed Maurice instead, who picked up instantly.

"Yes, sir?"

"Don't call me sir, please. Did the boys eat?"

"Yes, sir."

"I said..." *Sigh.* Some things just weren't worth the fight. "Great, thank you. What's on their schedules today?"

A slight pause and ruffle of papers. "Floyd has therapy at nine for two hours, and Theo has hockey practice at the same time. After that, they're free. Most Saturdays Hank would take them sailing after that."

Daven groaned. He was *not* going sailing, end of story. "I didn't know Theo plays hockey. With who?"

"Well, he has private lessons at the country club. Hank won't let him play on a team yet, although he's quite good. It's a bit of a security issue."

The thought of Theo playing a team sport completely by himself depressed Daven inexpressibly, and he resolved to fix that right away. The boy needed companionship and friends.

"Right. Can you give me a list of all the youth teams in the area and contact numbers for them?"

"I already have such a list, sir. I'll print it for you immediately."

"Just email it to me." Daven gave his email address. "Listen, I want to ask you something. Last night Floyd mentioned that Chef should have been in Eagle Rock. Was that true?"

"Uh, yes, sir. The servants go home on Friday afternoons."

Daven bristled a little, but then backed off just as quickly. He didn't want to start off on the wrong foot with this man, who was obviously just trying to do his best under very trying circumstances.

"Okay. You need to tell me these things in the future," he said, trying his best to keep the statement from sounding like a reprimand. "I'm kind of running blind, here. I have no idea how Hank runs his household."

"Sorry, sir. I just assumed...I mean, you've known him for so long, and the boys...I thought you would fit right in without any guidance."

Fit right in. Hardly. "I'm afraid that's not the case." Daven felt himself soften up suddenly. "Listen, let's have lunch together today and talk about this. I need all the help I can get, and your input will be invaluable."

"Certainly, sir. What would you like to eat so I can obtain the ingredients this morning?"

"No, I mean at a restaurant. I have a list of ones with private rooms that I'll email you."

There was a shocked silence. "Sir, I can't...I'm indentured, I can't be seen...it's not proper."

Daven sighed. "I don't care. Pick a restaurant and let me know so I can call and make a reservation."

Another shocker. "But I...I'll make the reservation, of course. Sir, are you sure about this?"

Maurice sounded rather shaky, and even though Daven detested the indentured system and the societal imbalances it created, he knew he was making the poor man highly uncomfortable and that it would help to take a more authoritative stance.

"Yes," he amended, "you should make the reservation, of course, and arrange for transportation. Who is the weekend driver?"

"Vance is always here on the weekends for the family. I mean…for you and the boys, sir."

The family.

Daven swallowed hard again. "Great. We'll eat at noon at King's Head, if they have a room available. Let me know. Gather whatever lists and information you think is of the highest priority for me to know first."

"Yes, sir. And what will the boys do while we're gone?"

Oh, right, the boys…it's not just me anymore. Get your shit together, Daven.

"Have they been to the Getty?"

"No, sir."

"Okay. They'll go there. I'll arrange it with Brittany."

"An *art museum* ? Is he serious?" Floyd whined as wrangled the polo shirt off over his head and looked for something else to wear, per Daven's instructions. "And I have to freakin' dress up?"

"Not dress up," Maurice corrected. "But something nicer than a polo shirt. Slacks and a dress shirt will be fine."

He went into Theo's room and found the boy already dressed exactly correct, of course.

"I've been wanting to go to this place for months!" Theo exclaimed happily. "How did he know?"

"He probably heard it from your dad. Are you ready to go?"

"Yeah."

"Okay, the car is outside. Have fun."

Maurice went back into Floyd's room and found him in the same state as before - but now holding clothes in each hand - shirtless, pouting, and in no mood to go anywhere.

"Floyd, the car is outside waiting."

"I don't care. I'm not going." He jumped a little as the sound of Daven coming up the stairs reached his ears. "Maurice? Tell him I'm not going."

"Yes, you are," said Daven gravely as he stood in the doorway. "The shirt you're holding in your right hand is fine. Put it on, and let's go."

Maurice was astonished to see Floyd drop them both on the floor and turn defiantly away from Daven to sit on the bed. "No."

"Floyd," pleaded Maurice quietly, almost a whisper. "Don't. Your dad wouldn't want this."

"He's not here," Floyd shot back, glaring at Daven at the same time.

Daven, of course, had no idea why Floyd had suddenly taken such a disliking to him. It hurt, but he kept a straight face.

"Would you like to come to lunch with me and Maurice instead? We're going to be discussing how your dad runs the household, and how we should proceed from here on out if he doesn't return. Your opinion matters, and I'd like to hear it."

Once again, Floyd was completely thrown off by Daven asking him for his opinion outright, rather than launching straight into a fight. It was so completely different from his dad. But then again, maybe his dad would still be here if it wasn't for Daven.

"He's going to return, so you're wasting your time," Floyd blurted out, even knowing it wasn't true. He had somehow already accepted he wouldn't see his dad again for a while, but it felt good anyway to say he'd be back.

Daven entered the room and looked at Maurice. "I think we need a moment, if you please." Then, to Floyd after they were alone: "Floyd, you know your dad's in trouble. We talked about this already, and he even told you that himself. I can't just take over this household without any kind of guidance, whether it's for five days or five years. You and Theo need stability, and so do I. Now, do you want to go to lunch with us, or do you want to go to the art museum? There is no third choice."

"I'm not going anywhere," Floyd insisted quietly. Just as he said that, his phone rang with his dad's ringtone. He bolted away from Daven and snatched it off the bathroom counter.

"Dad!"

"Hey, kiddo. How are you doing?"

"Not good. Daven is trying to make me go to an art museum!" Floyd whined again.

"Really? The Getty? You should go, it's really cool. We had a company holiday party there last year. Theo's been wanting to go forever."

Floyd glanced back at Dav. "Dad, I really want to talk to you… *alone*," he added significantly.

"Alright, call me when you get home."

"But I don't want to go."

Hank chuckled a little. "That's what I said, too. Like father, like son. Look, I can't talk right now anyway. I just called to say hi. When you get home around six I'll have all the time in the world, okay? Call me then. Don't miss the room with all the Rawson tapestries. Some of them are over a thousand years old."

"*Rawson tapestries*. Oh my god, dad. You're such a nerd." Floyd smiled, then gave in at last. A thousand years old sounded pretty cool, actually. "Alright, I'll go. I'll call you at six, okay? Isn't that late over there?"

"Nope. I'll be just starting my day at this rate. Talk to you then, son. Love you."

"Love you too, dad."

Floyd waited until his dad hung up, then he slowly picked his shirt up off the floor and put it on. Daven was no longer in the room, and Floyd hadn't noticed when he left. So he walked down to the car alone and shoved Theo over as he got in.

"Hey! Sit in the back, asshole," Theo protested.

"We can both fit here, bitch," Floyd replied grumpily, with another shove.

"Not if you keep eating as much bacon as you did this morning," Theo shot back with a firm shove of his own.

"Boys," warned Brittany calmly, although she wanted to laugh instead.

"Sorry," the brothers mumbled together.

The car pulled away from the driveway and into the street. From the passenger seat mirror Brittany pretended not to see Floyd suddenly put an arm protectively around his brother and pull him close. Theo squirmed away in silent protest at first, but then changed his mind and went back in for a re-do. Floyd draped an arm around him again, and covered them both up to their shoulders with the car's resident cashmere blanket.

The boys were quiet and still all the way to the museum.

CHAPTER SIX

Tuesday, March 28

Mayfair Federal Prison - Negotiating Room

"Fine. I'm not walking away. I have the official offer here." Lester laid out four pages on the table and shoved it through the tiny little crack on the table to the other side of the wire partition. "As the interested party, the Urbanes decide the penalty. If you confess to all charges and agree to be executed, then Harmon will deed-"

"*Executed?* What the holy fuck?" Hank nearly screeched. He swiped all the papers off the table with both hands and jumped up. Lester calmly continued

"-as I was saying, Harmon will deed your sons to my training school for nine months. I don't have to tell you that I'll take excellent care of them, but saying it anyway just in case you've forgotten how much they mean to me."

"What about me? Do I mean nothing to you?" Hank demanded. "I can't believe you bought into this Urbanes brainwashing shit."

Lester stared at him. "I'm not an Urbane anymore. I'm an Independent who works for an Urbanes-funded organization, like thousands of others. And I'm not here for you."

Hank answered quickly, and firmly, gesturing wildly around the room as he did so. "So this isn't about me, Lester? Are you serious? This is all about me and the knowledge I have of

Harmon's crimes. He's asking me to trade my life for…for…you haven't seen my sons in ten years. You don't know them. They won't even *know* you . Floyd might, but Theo definitely won't. He was only two. And even if Floyd does remember, the last time we were together, you had a shotgun pointed at my chest. You think he's just going to let that go?"

Lester shrugged. "You do have that effect on people."

"So I just have to confess to everything, huh? That's your idea of justice?"

"You're guilty as sin, Hank, and everyone knows it. Time to think of the boys now."

"They're *all* I'm thinking about, Lester! Floyd is already 16. I can't believe you, of all people….no. I'm not signing anything." Hank was almost in tears, which is extremely rare for him. "Leave me the fuck alone. Maybe I should have been the one threatening to kill *you* ten years ago. And maybe I should have done it."

"Hank," warned Lester in a low tone. "Calm down."

Hank fixed him with an astonished expression. "Easy for you to say."

"This isn't my doing. This is Harmon, and you need to agree to it," Lester said placidly. "For the boys. You have no other option. You're already nailed with blackmail and that's a five year sent-"

"I know that. Goddamn, stop repeating yourself." Hank turned his back to Lester and drummed his fingers on his hips impatiently. "Harmon isn't the only one who can propose terms for this plea bargain. I want to talk to him."

"You can't."

"Fuck you. I can, and I will. Arrange it for the sake of Floyd and Theo. Or else what happens next is your fault."

Lester scoffed. "Nothing you could say would make me think that."

Hank turned around, eyed him dangerously, then smirked. "Oh Lester, you know I love a challenge. So here's the deal: arrange for me to speak to Harmon today, or be prepared to live with yourself when my boys are separated forever. Because that'll all be on you, I guarantee it. I'll do it. I'll let this fall apart, just to make a point. I *know* you. It will *break* you to have that on your conscience."

Lester breathed hard for a few long moments. "You're a...you haven't changed a bit, let's just put it that way."

"But you have, Lester. And I hate what I'm seeing. Do the right thing and give me at least a glimpse of the man who I fought with side by side through the years of the revolution. He's got to still be in there somewhere. I have faith."

Lester's eyes narrowed dangerously. "You've never had faith in anything, asshole."

The smile was gone now. "Well, maybe I *have* changed, then. But at least it's for the better, which is more than I can say for you."

Hank sat back down and crossed his arms, glaring at Lester with conviction and daring.

Lester sighed. "Fine. I'll see what I can do. For Floyd and Theo, not for you."

Hank wasn't granted the call with Harmon. He fully expected that and didn't blame Lester, however. Instead, he asked to call Daven and was granted the request. He was taken to a private room in the jail's offices for the task.

"I want my guard to be on the call as well," he told Stewart firmly. It wasn't a question. "He's going to start looking after Daven now, and I want to tell them both what my next steps are."

Stewart looked at Avery, then nodded. "I don't see why not. Come with me. You have 15 minutes."

"Thank you ever so much for your kindness," Hank replied facetiously, with a mock bow. "Avery, come on."

"Boss? What do you mean I'm going to-"

"Shhh." He shut the door of the little room behind him and watched Stewart settle in the room next door, purposefully keeping his back to the glass.

"Give me your phone," Hank whispered.

"What? Sir-"

"Your phone. Take mine and call Daven, but tell him to hold in silence until I'm done with this call. Mute us. Don't disconnect the line."

"Hank, no. You can't," Avery protested, having realized in dismay what his rebellious boss was up to.

"Do it, or fly back to Los Angeles today and leave me to fend for myself. Your choice."

Avery grumbled and rolled his eyes a little, but he finally took the proffered phone and handed Hank his own.

"Good afternoon," Hank began formally a few moments later, not sure whether to be relieved or not that his rival actually picked up the phone. It might have been better if he didn't. "I hope your day is going a lot better than mine."

"Holy shit," Harmon replied in shock. "You just don't know how to give up, do you? Goodbye."

"Okay. Guess you'll never know what I'm about to tell you, then. Too bad." Hank sighed dramatically, then paused as he heard Avery quietly explain to Daven why he was calling, and he almost missed Harmon's reply.

"-balls to call me again?" asked Harmon in wonder, and not a little admiration. "Only you would think you can get away with this."

"That's the goal. My charm and wit goes a long way, you know. I'll bet you $100 you don't report me."

"You know I won't," the other man responded, his tone more puzzled than usual. "You're in enough trouble already."

"That didn't stop you from reporting me the first time," Hank nearly spat back.

"Well, I was pissed off because I'd just found out Janet was the one who leaked our info."

Hank paused, wanting to scoff at that nonsense, but realizing it would get him absolutely nowhere at the moment. The last thing he needed was to lose the chance to have one final word with Harmon.

"Are you alone?" Hank asked carefully.

"Yes. Are you?"

"Obviously. Stewart thinks I'm calling Daven." Hank said a quick prayer under his breath. "Look, I know you're trying to help. The FBI has made it clear to me that without agreeing to a plea with you, this trial will never be wrapped up in time. I understand it was your idea to push it along faster to help out the boys."

There was the sound of a cleared throat from the other line, twice. "Not exactly my idea, no."

"Right. Anyway, I just want to know why you're pushing for execution. Do I really scare you that much?"

Harmon was obviously incredibly uncomfortable; Hank could hear him shifting in his chair. "I was advised that you confessing to all charges was the fastest way to wrap up the trial. Some of those charges require capital punishment. It's an ugly situation Hank, but you have to admit that you pretty much brought it on yourself."

Hank's heart raced at that. "Ah. So you think I'm guilty, then. Corporate espionage, Janet's murder, that big whole list."

"I'm not sure about Janet's murder. I've asked for it to be removed from consideration. But everything else? Absolutely. I have no doubt. If I did-"

"Of course you're not sure about Janet," Hank laughed harshly. "Because *you* did it. You, and Colbert, and some unknown motherfucker in my organization-"

"Hank-"

"-and I think you're afraid I'll find proof of it. That's why you want me gone. I see right you through you, my friend. You're more transparent than Saran Wrap."

Harmon ignored this line of questioning and went a different direction entirely. "Let's forget about Janet for a moment. I'm doing what I'm doing to help your sons, not you. I don't care what happens to you."

"You don't say."

"But I'm willing to sweeten the pot a bit if it helps."

"How on earth do you sweeten a pot of shit?" Hank asked with another dark chuckle. "The answer is no, I'm not agreeing to a fucking thing. You're scared because you *know* my informants gave me a lot of ammunition. I may be making you a plea bargain of my own if they can get their dossier together fast enough. But if not. Daven will take you down for me, and he'll have all the time in the world to do it. You are just as fucked as I am, my friend."

That seemed to set Harmon back on his heels, and Hank heard his quick intake of breath. "Okay, Hank. You like to say you're a realist. So let's get real. Even if I dropped my case and went down on charges myself, the FBI isn't going to stop their pursuit of you. Five years in jail, *minimum* , Hank, for what they've proven already."

"I'll take it. Maybe you and I will be cellmates. Wouldn't that be fun?"

Harmon's tone went dark; he was no longer in the mood for Hank's bullying. "Fine. Let me put it another way. Let's see what happens if you don't agree to a plea. Take me out of the picture entirely, Hank, and your boys go away for life because the FBI cannot wrap this up by March 31. But I can get it done with this plea bargain. Floyd and Theo? I'm their savior. You should be *grateful* that I'm offering to trade your life for theirs. Not threatening me."

"You're right. I'll send you a thank you card from death row."

Harmon ignored that, his blood now boiling. "And to get more *real* - you know who forced me to pursue the blackmail charge on you and offer a plea bargain? Stewart. I wanted to do this in civil court. He is literally the reason we're talking right now. When this all came up, I was only looking forward to suing you and making a nice chunk of change from that tape."

Hank's throat went dry, and his lungs started to hurt. "That's bullshit," he croaked without conviction.

"No, it's not. But everything you've said is. I'm done with this conversation. Goodbye."

"*Wait* . Just...wait." He was relieved to still hear breathing on the other line. "What is this... *sweetening the pot* you were talking about?" he asked quietly, carefully.

A long pause in which Hank was afraid Harmon had cut the connection, then a heavy sigh. "This has to remain between you and me. I can't put it in writing…but I guarantee you I will transfer Floyd and Theo's deed to Daven after the one-year waiting period."

No answer.

"Hank?" Harmon pressed after a minute.

"I'm here. If you're feeling so charitable, why don't you just transfer them to him right away?" he asked skeptically.

"You know why. Daven is under investigation, too. If he gets hit with a felony…and even if he doesn't, the courts can pull it back. It honestly makes no sense for me to do that, regardless. The public will see it as a bribe to get you to plead guilty, and the last thing I need right now is another PR nightmare at the hands of the Seditionists."

Hank closed his eyes and suddenly felt like a runaway train was barreling straight at him. "Fuck me, this is out of control. You know what, though? If you hadn't given them that tape recording, I'd still be free!"

Harmon refused to feel guilty about that. "For now. You're lucky I did. As I said, Stewart knew it was the only way to-"

"What else do they have on me?" Hank asked offhandedly. "I mean…this is…"

"Have you not seen the list of charges yet?"

"Of course I have." Hank rubbed his temples. "So I'm fucked, is what you're saying. You think Daven won't be approved."

"Correct. The courts can't risk it. I have nothing to do with the Daven issue, so you can take that up with him."

Harmon was right. Hank felt like he was going to throw up. He had to agree to the plea.

It was over.

It was well and truly over.

He was going to die within the week.

"Okay, so…" Hank took a deep, steady breath despite the jangling of his nerves. "You do realize you're going to turn out to be the villain in this scenario, right? The public is going to hate you. And the Urbanes."

"No. The terms of the plea bargain will remain confidential for ten years. That's one of the caveats. Your kids are stuck with me for a year, whether you like it or not.

Stuck with Harmon. Well, considering Daven's cavalier behavior lately, this might be the better option, Hank thought darkly.

"So what happens to them during the twelve months?"

"Already worked it out," Harmon continued brightly, heartened by the fact that Hank was finally seeing the light. "They can go to Lester Boyd's school for 9 months, then work for three months in a home of my choosing. After that…well, they become Daven's servants for the next 19 years. And we both know he won't treat them like actual servants."

Hank rubbed his temples yet again. "I can't believe this shit."

"Hank, even as much as you hate me, you know I would *never* do anything to harm your children. They'll be in good hands."

Hank knew it was true, as much as he hated this man. "What kind of school is it?"

"House servant training. Top tier, safest bet there is. And it will keep them together for the entire term of their indenture...even if something happens to Daven."

"That works," Hank said quickly, not really believing this was even happening and that he was even speaking such words. His eyes were still closed, his head throbbing in pain. "But I want their deed to go to Lester. Not you. And I want this entire agreement in writing. Verbal is not enough."

Harmon was puzzled. "Lester *Boyd* ? That's, uh...under what rationale?"

"Under the rationale that I don't trust your sorry ass."

"And you trust *him* that much?"

"With them, I do." It wasn't quite the truth; Hank didn't really trust Lester either, but he was enormously worried Harmon would lose the deeds if he was taken down by Daven and Rupert. Not if... *when* . Because after his best friends found out about his death and figured out what had gone down in Philadelphia, it was over for Harmon, too. Lester was the safest bet.

"That makes no sense. I'm the one who's trying to help them," Harmon added, still puzzled.

"They go to Lester, or you can hit me with another blackmail charge in about five seconds," Hank threatened icily, although it was all for nothing, really. His informants had almost nothing at all to go with, to his great disappointment. But Harmon didn't know that, so he wasted no time grabbing at the opportunity to get them out of the picture.

"Agreed, then. Looks like I picked the right negotiator after all."

Hank was silent for a long time, and Harmon didn't prompt him.

Eventually Harmon said, "Well…I'm going to revise the draft of the plea bargain and send it back to Stewart for your review. I hope you take it, Hank. There's not much time to keep fighting about it."

"You're telling me. Before I go," Hank continued, "I'm going to give you some priceless advice for free: get rid of Colbert. He's been playing you like a fiddle all along. Dump his ass now, or you're going to be next to fall."

"Really. And what evidence do you have, exactly?"

Hank cut him off firmly. "Let's just say I'm so certain he's behind this, that I don't blame you for this situation. I'm not even mad. Ten years ago when I visited Colbert in prison, he vowed to do the same for me. Now he's come to collect on that promise. My time is up."

"He…*what* are you talking about?" Harmon queried, genuinely bewildered.

Hank ignored the question. "Good luck if you decide to ignore my warning. You're going to need it."

Harmon closed his eyes and took a deep breath. "Hank, just so you know. I never wanted-"

The line disconnected, and Harmon slowly opened his eyes to the sight of the phone trembling slightly in his hand. In the background, through the glass, Colbert slowly came into focus. He was standing by the coffee maker with Zane, bantering and grinning like he didn't have a care in the world.

Harmon watched him for a long moment, then pushed the dark thoughts aside and pulled up the plea bargain document on his laptop.

"Hank?" prompted Avery quietly. Hank took his phone back with a gulp and hung up on Daven without a word.

"Avery...I..."

"This is bullshit," Avery said plainly, and he yanked his phone out of Hank's hands and left the room angrily. Hank followed him silently, feeling like a child trailing an angry parent. Stewart was waiting at the table, watching them curiously.

"May we continue?" he asked calmly. "Or do you two need a minute?"

"We're good," said Avery tightly, ignoring the piercing glare Hank shot him. "I'll go back out the lobby if there's nothing else."

He didn't wait for either man to answer and simply walked right out the door, slamming it hard behind him.

"Okay then," Stewart said after an awkward pause. "You want to go after him, or-"

"No. Thanks." Hank sat down hard and dutifully handed his phone to Stewart, who scrolled through the call log. He spotted the 7-minute call to Daven, and handed the phone back.

"Thanks. On second thought, bring Avery back in here please."

"Why?"

"Just do it. Now, if you please."

Hank got up, his heart pounding. What the hell was Stewart going to... *oh, shit.* He stuck his head out the door and Avery came in immediately, still ablaze with fury.

Stewart stood up and put a hand out.

"Your phone, please."

Avery threw him a blank look. "My phone? Why?"

"I want to see the call log, if you please. Although it's not actually a request."

Hank sucked in his breath and struggled to keep a neutral expression.

"Yes, sir." Avery reluctantly dug his phone out of his inner pocket and handed it over.

"Thank you," Stewart said, somewhat sheepishly. He scrolled through the list very briefly, and then handed it back. "Sorry, I'm just doing my job. Thank you."

Avery nodded and left after cocking an eyebrow at his boss. Hank was astonished that Stewart continued the conversation as if nothing untoward had occurred…it just wasn't possible that he hadn't seen the call to Harmon. It was even more impossible for him to ignore it, if he had seen it.

Hank could hardly concentrate on Stewart's words as he was escorted back to the portico into a waiting car, and during the long ride to the hotel, he kept his face carefully expressionless in order to not give away that he was royally pissed off with the man for forcing Harmon into this situation…even though he was doing it to help Hank.

Hank was immensely relieved to finally be dropped off at the hotel and glanced at Avery with a look that clearly said "follow me, " but he was ignored. So instead of going to his own room, he boldly followed Avery into his and slammed the door behind them.

"If you have something to say, just say it," he challenged irritably.

Avery threw his boss a glare that all but set the room on fire. "Actually, no. I have zero desire to talk to you right now."

"What the hell?" Hank exclaimed in surprise as he followed his guard to the far side of the room, running both hands through his hair in frustration all the while. "Then just answer one question and I'll go. How did Stewart not see that call?"

Avery was breathing heavily as he continued to throw eye daggers at his boss. "Did you really not know that I carry two phones? One for work, one for personal?"

"No. I didn't know that." The realization then hit him like a brick in the face, and his heart raced a little as he stared at Avery's back. "Oh, shit. So you handed him the wrong phone."

"The *right* phone, you mean. You're welcome."

Hank's head was swimming a little. Actually, quite a lot. His tongue felt three times thicker than usual, too. It was a close call... *way* too close.

"Jesus Christ on a pogo stick. Avery, I can't tell you how grateful I am for your-"

"Don't bother, Hank. I quit," Avery said simply, without any heat.

"Avery!" Hank gasped.

Avery crossed his arms and kept his tone steady. "You acted unethically and put me in danger - and not the physical kind, which is the *only* kind I agreed to when I signed up for this job. So I consider this a breach of contract and expect an appropriate severance package."

Hank had never known Avery to be even half as angry at him before, and he was shocked into speechlessness at this declaration. He held up his hands in a *seriously* ? gesture and stared open-mouthed, feeling indignant and crushed all at once.

Avery was suddenly outwardly serene again, but an emotional explosion was simmering just below the surface as he crossed the room to the other side and yanked his suitcase out of the closet. "I'll stay here long enough for my replacement to arrive. Who do you want me to send over, sir?"

"Deveraux," Hank croaked after a moment. "I'll arrange it. You need to relax."

"I'm fine, and I'll take care of it. He should be able to make the 9pm flight and be here by dawn."

Hank felt his heart rise into his throat and stick there nauseatingly.

"Thanks." Hank noticed his hands were shaking, which irritated him even more. "You're right, I acted in an unforgivable manner. But may I ask why you're so furious that you want to just walk away? It seems out of proportion, no offense."

Avery did not waver. "Because I couldn't remember which pocket held which phone, and nearly had a heart attack on the spot trying to remember. It was sheer luck I grabbed the right one, but if Stewart finds out what I did…like I said, I didn't sign up for this."

He turned and jerked opened the suitcase and laid it open on the bed. Hank kept quiet for a minute while the man angrily threw all his belongings in, then spoke again quietly during a break in the furor.

"I'm sorry, Avery. I accept your resignation, since you insisted. But please reconsider. We've been friends for six years; don't let it end like this."

"No, I'm your employee and nothing more. *Former* employee, as of tomorrow."

Ouch , Hank thought with a sharp pang to his heart. It was a well-deserved jibe, but still. He softened his tone down to one he almost never used, except with Floyd when he needed soothing.

"Hey," he began impulsively, hesitantly. "Stop what you're doing for a second and talk to me. *Please* . It's important. Just...one more minute of your time is the last thing I'll ever ask of you."

Avery did stop, obviously deeply concerned about Hank's unusual pleading tone.

"Yes?" he asked with a visible degree of trepidation.

Hank wandered over the bed and sat down, defeated and tired. He reached back to grab one of the pillows and put it over his lap as if it could offer some kind of comfort and protection.

"Listen, Avery...I, uh..." His voice cracked briefly and he had to take a moment to regroup. "I'm not going home. This is it."

"Yeah, I gathered that."

Hank gripped the pillow tighter. "I need...I'm *asking* you to stay and take really good care of Dav. Please."

Avery wasn't moved. "He has his own guard already. As for that conversation with Harmon. I only heard part of it, not enough to piece together all that's going on. But it sounded to me like you were negotiating a prison sentence with him."

"Yeah, I was," Hank lied.

"Prison," Avery repeated flatly. "You said you were innocent."

"Look, it's complicated. I can't get into it. But this trip to Philadelphia has turned a one-way ticket, and that's the ugly truth. Will you stay with Daven? He will need you. I'll have your contract turned over to him tomorrow if you agree."

Avery just stared, his body at a complete standstill and his face frozen into an expression of disbelief.

Hank stood up and gently put the pillow back in place. "I'm sorry, this is a lot to take in without warning. I'm truly sorry about the phone thing. Honestly I had no choice, though, and I'd do it again if I had to. Hate me if you want, but it's the truth. Let me know in the morning what you decide."

Avery cleared his throat twice before responding. "I don't need time. The answer is no. But with your permission I'd like to stop by and say goodbye to the boys tomorrow."

The boys. Oh god . Hank had no intention of telling Avery what was going to happen to them; obviously the poor man hadn't heard enough of the conversation to realize the deeds he kept referring to were Floyd and Theo's. He must have thought Hank was referring to transferring the house servants, since everyone on the planet knew that Daven was the Bancroft boys' next guardian.

"Of course you can see them. And visit them whenever." Hank was suddenly exhausted. "But don't bother calling Martinez. You and Brody can fly home together tomorrow at noon. I won't be needing a guard or a lawyer any longer than that."

CHAPTER SEVEN

FBI Headquarters - FBI

Tuesday evening

It wasn't often that Stewart was left dumbfounded by new developments (after all, six years on the front lines in the Army tended to leave one nearly immune to surprises in later life), but he was entirely numb after he read Harmon's plea bargain. Salome was in a meeting, so he picked up the phone and called the leader of the Urbanes after he was finished digesting the new terms. Well, perhaps *digesting* was the wrong word.

"Harmon. Stewart. Listen, uh...what on earth went down between Mr. Boyd and Hank? I've just read his alleged agreement to these terms."

"Not alleged," Harmon corrected. "He did agree to them, and those were the amendments he wanted."

"How do you know that? I just left him an hour ago and he hadn't made any decision yet. He made it clear he had no interest in continuing any further negotiations with you."

Harmon cleared his throat roughly; being just as forbidden to talking to Hank as the reverse, he wasn't willing to admit his part in the affair.

"Well, maybe he just needed time to think."

Stewart set his coffee down hard, the realization behind's Harmon's caginess slamming him in the chest like a kick. "You two did talk. I *knew* it. And you told him."

"Told him what?"

"That I'm behind this. You did. Or Lester Boyd did. Don't lie. That's the only reason why he would have clammed up on me so quickly, and with such hostility. Because he never needs *time to think* , as you put it. The man makes massive decisions at the blink of an eye, always has. You know that."

Harmon swallowed hard. "I told him nothing. Lester might have."

"Bullshit. I can see right through you, even over the phone."

"No, you can't, because you're wrong. Can we please go over the document now?"

Stewart threw the papers down. "Oh sure, no problem. You just want Hank to die, is all. No big deal, let's just get it over with, huh?"

"Did you just call me to bitch me out, or are we going to get some actual work done here?"

"We're not doing a damned thing until you tell me if you spoke to him today. Yes, or no?"

Harmon gritted his teeth. "No. Why don't you ask him, if you're so sure? You know he can't lie."

"You're correct. Hold on."

Stewart pressed down the hold button with an angry jab, then set the phone on the desk and got up to pace his office. The truth was, he didn't want to confirm that Hank and Harmon spoke. If he didn't hear it directly, he didn't have to report it. He waited a few minutes to give himself time to breathe and calm down, then picked the receiver back up again.

"Alright, you two didn't speak. My apologies. Let's go over these terms, one by one. Starting with the corporate espionage confession..."

Hilton Philadelphia

Late evening

Lester Boyd couldn't sleep. Hank hadn't changed a bit, no. But his comments about the way *Lester* had changed was really driving him to distraction. The two men had lived one of those dangerously special kinds of friendships, where they each knew too much about the other. That was never a good position for two men of strong opinion and fiery temperament. As such, they had parted ways ten years ago knowing they were equally doomed if one turned on the other. So they hadn't done that.

Until now...Lester had been the one to turn on Hank this time. He had reason; the man broke every law in the spectrum and had somehow become a bigger asshole than he was before. Hell, he'd even threatened to separate his own children just to make life all that much harder for Lester. Hank deserved to go down.

So why couldn't Lester Boyd sleep? He didn't want Hank to die, for the boys' sake. Their grief would ultimately lie at the feet of the man who convinced Hank that death was the right decision. And that man was Lester. So he knew, even now, that his own life would forever be plagued with the guilt he had been so desperately trying to avoid earlier today.

Hank Bancroft had won. Again.

He didn't know at this time, of course, that it was all Harmon's doing. Or more accurately, Colbert. He wouldn't find out for a while; it would be months before his world turned upside down for a third time. In the meantime, he emptied the contents of his hotel room's minibar and finally passed out asleep at 4am Wednesday morning.

Ritz-Carlton Philadelphia

4am Wednesday morning

I don't wish for you to blame yourself in any way. I'm not convinced that the Seditionists are on the right path, and it would-

Hank scratched out these sentences for the fourth time and began again.

The Seditionists, under my direction, has lost our way over the past year. I'm counting on you to bring us back to a place where we can think again of the best interests of all citizens, not just our own constituents. While I wish for Harmon to be

*removed at your hands, you cannot let the effort obsess you
and-*

Obsess you. No...preoccupy?

*-overtake your efforts to re-establish a firm hold on proper
morals and ethics. Therefore, it is under my express
command that you hold off from-*

Hank tore up the entire paper and sighed in frustration and
anger. This flowery language was not his specialty, and he
needed to be more direct with this particular recipient, who
wouldn't be impressed by being forced to read between the
lines. He grabbed a fresh sheet of paper, and as an
afterthought exchanged his black pen for a blue one in the
hopes that would somehow help sweep away his writer's block.

Dav,

*I'm sorry we didn't get to speak again before my death.
Honestly, I wouldn't have known what to say. That I fucked
up? That you and the boys have to pay the price for that?
That I probably destroyed everything we've accomplished?
How do I even possibly start to make amends? The answer is
retribution, with my own life. Forgive me for taking the
coward's way out.*

*I know the Seditionists are in good hands with you and
Rupert, but you have to keep in mind that bringing down
Harmon isn't your first priority. Getting us back to a position
of trust and esteem must take precedence over everything
else. Your constituents are counting on you to put them first.
Hell, the entire nation expects that. And you must put them
first. Always.*

When you get custody of the boys on April 1 next year, be prepared for them to be very different than they were before. Floyd's going to be angry. Theo's going to be even angrier. They may hate you. They will probably hate me. All I can say is, they love their Uncle Dav and will come around eventually. Have patience and treat them with more understanding and gentleness than I ever did. Floyd will test you until you're ready to have a nervous breakdown, and Theo? Well, he's young. He has no filter and no stop button. But you do. Use them generously.

In my plea bargain agreement, which is sealed for ten years, I took all responsibility for the recent errors in judgment you committed under my watch. That's why you were pardoned unconditionally. Just don't make any further mistakes, because I can't protect you a second time.

That being said, always remember that none of what happened to me was ultimately your fault. I chose to live my life on the razor's edge, and always knew the consequences could be dire. I'm at peace with the knowledge that my legacy will live on through the great things you and I accomplished together over the past decade.

Farewell, my loyal friend. See you on the other side...

Hank

PS

Really got to work on your people skills. Still rusty.

Hank didn't read the letter a second time for errors or clarity. He couldn't. His eyes were tired, and rapidly filling up with moisture. He folded up the paper and carefully slid it into the envelope, but didn't seal it yet. Stewart said he would have to read it first to make sure nothing in it would cause further legal problems with Daven.

Setting that letter aside, he swung his chair around to the other side of the desk and picked up the plea bargain that had been delivered by courier almost 6 hours ago. He'd hadn't signed it yet, because he was planning to demand to meet with Lester one more time in the morning. He'd say it was for a clarification, but in truth, he just wanted to be able to confront the man about his part in this and rub salt in the wound one last time.

Eventually Hank realized he didn't want to read that either and folded it up, too, forcing himself to stop thinking about all of this for at least a minute. So he took a shower and started to go to sleep as the sun was just starting to tug at the very edges of the horizon.

Then he realized he might not ever have another chance to see that sight, so he dragged himself to the reading chair by the window and watched Philadelphia transition from black and white into full color.

Anyone else would have winced at the thought of Independence Hall being the last thing he saw before he closed his eyes to rest, but Hank always did appreciate the black humor in such irony. There was a smile on his lips as he drifted off to sleep in the big fluffy chair that reminded him fondly of the one at the office Daven had hated so much and threatened to torch in Rupert's front yard.

CHAPTER EIGHT

Seditionists Headquarters

Friday, March 31

"Daven... *Daven* ." Billie waited a moment more, then cleared her throat loudly. "Mr. Johansson."

"*What* ?" Dav looked up from his notebook at last. He was in a rare temper, and everyone at the office had been afraid to set foot within 20 feet of him all day. Even Rupert.

"A gentleman is here to see you. Won't tell me his name, but he says-"

Daven stood up upon spying a familiar face peeking around the corner at him. "Thank you, Billie. Come in, Stewart. Shut the door. Why didn't you tell me you were coming?"

"I couldn't. I'm sorry."

Stewart sat down, looking for all the world like he would rather be anywhere else. Inside of an active volcano, perhaps. Daven's heart dropped a little.

"What news of Hank?" he demanded roughly; Hank's comments on his rusty people skills were the last thing on his priority list right now.

"Nice to see you, too. Alright, let's get down to it. I can't tell you anything unless you sign a confidentiality agreement that binds you and the Seditionists organization to permanent media silence on the topic of Hank's trial and outcome."

"Permanent!" exclaimed Daven furiously. "That's bullshit. What kind of idiot yahoo thought I would agree to that?"

Stewart's eyes narrowed. "I did, or I wouldn't have flown all the way out here. Calm down, Mr. Johansson. You need to come with me. My car is waiting-"

"No. I would show you out, but I'm very busy. Goodbye."

Stewart fully expected this; his tone remained steady and placating. "Fine. I can see you're under a tremendous amount of stress and not open to suggestion. So let me switch to facts. If you *don't* come with me, you're going to be very unpleasantly surprised and confused when you get home. Show me out, please."

Daven fixed him with an icy glare. "You know the way."

"Do it anyway. I won't ask again. You might want to pack up for the day."

Daven froze, hearing the warning in his tone. "Will I...will I be able to come back tomorrow?"

" *Yes* . You aren't being arrested. My sincerest apologies if I gave that impression."

"But the boys are expecting me home in an hour-"

"*Daven* ," Stewart snapped as he stood up, not willing to argue any further. "Let's go."

There was something in his tone now that made Daven comply, despite every desire to the contrary. He remembered Hank's words from a recent conversation: *Stewart has always been a friend to me...do as he says* . So Daven got up reluctantly, gathered his things, put on his coat, and quietly walked the man out the door and down the hallway to the elevator.

Stewart whispered. "We're going to Hank's house. Just get in the car and don't make a fuss. Don't even talk. Understood?"

Daven stared at him, bitterly swallowing the automatic protest. "Yes, understood."

"Thank you."

Daven was not just unpleasantly surprised when they arrived at the Bancroft house; he was astonished. Every single member of the household staff and guards were waiting at the door in terrified silence. He spun around to Stewart in bewilderment as they walked down the long hallway to the study.

"What the hell is going on?" Daven demanded in front of the entire FBI entourage that had followed them into the house from three different cars.

"We'll talk in a moment," Stewart replied coldly as he reached into his jacket pocket. "This conversation will be recorded for the protection of both of us. Will you come with-"

" No ."

"Come with me, Mr. Johansson. My group will stay out here." Stewart all but shoved Daven into the study and then slammed the door behind him, after which he hissed forcefully, *"I'm on your side, for fuck's sake! Cooperate, damn it."*

He then set the recorder on the table with a flourish and jammed down the red button while glaring dangerously at Daven.

He raised his voice so it could be heard through the door. "Daven Johansson, I hereby inform you our conversation is now being recorded until I return to my car. You almost must sign this agreement before I can say anything more. Do you understand?"

"Yes, we're being recorded. Got it. I'm not signing a damned thing. What's going on?"

Stewart closed his eyes to the pain that was throbbing behind his eyeballs, and lowered his voice to a normal level. "If you don't *sign. the. agreement. I'll have to leave .*"

"Goodbye, then. Thanks for the ride home."

Stewart inched the paper closer to Daven and raised an eyebrow. "At least read it first. If you still don't agree, I'll go without another word."

Daven read the two paragraphs and was surprised to realize he didn't disagree with the reasoning behind the demand. The FBI simply wanted to control the messaging themselves to prevent both parties from savaging each other in the press. It wasn't a bad idea at all.

"Will Harmon have to sign this, too?"

"He already has, and he wasn't happy about it either. But do you understand why we're asking for this?"

Daven grabbed a pen and scrawled his name much larger and messier than normal.

"I have to admit it does make sense. Alright, I signed. Now talk."

"Thank you. Three days ago, Hank pled guilty to all charges. His sons are being indentured for twenty years as of tomorrow at noon. Do you understand?"

Daven's jaw fell open. "I......no. What? Are you serious?"

"Floyd and Theo were taken into the FBI's custody about an hour ago. That's why we're here."

Daven was thoroughly appalled. "You just...you just came in and *took them* ? Without notifying me first?"

"We had to. Hank wouldn't agree to it any other way."

Daven sat down hard. "He *agreed* to this? You've got to be fucking kidding me," he said, realizing at the same time how much he sounded like Hank in that moment. "This is...I can't...did he leave me any kind of explanation for all this?"

"Yes, actually. You'll be summoned to Philadelphia on June 15 to personally retrieve a letter he wrote you. I will also have more information to release to you at that time."

"Why would Hank make me wait so long?" Daven asked mildly. The fight in him was suddenly gone; he just wanted to talk now and was desperate to wake up from this nightmare.

"I can't say. I have on me the original paperwork Hank signed to transfer the boys' deeds to an anonymous party operative, as well as a copy of the charge sheet where he signed his name next to the guilty plea. You may view the documents now if you're in the right frame of mind."

Daven shook his head; not to say no, but in sheer disbelief. "He didn't do a damned thing. This was coerced out of him. Wasn't it?"

"A plea bargain is mutual coercement, technically. I think what you're asking is how do you know this signature is legit? That he wasn't under duress, or under threat if he didn't sign?"

"Yes," Dav answered shortly. Bitterly. "Exactly that. Show me, please."

Stewart did. "You will see they are all co-signed by myself and the president, as well as Salome Danby. The very reason I brought them with me was to assure you he wasn't forced into signing."

Daven parroted flatly as he handed the papers back, "So you're telling me the boys are...for twenty years..."

"Correct. Now, as you know, deeds can be transferred after one year, but until then they will be taken to a completely confidential location. Only five people will know where they are, and you cannot change that."

"Oh, really?" Daven replied sarcastically.

"Yes, really. I realize you could probably figure it out with all the people you know. But the terms of that confidentiality agreement you just signed strictly prohibits you from trying. Indirectly, that is."

Daven looked down to the paper, feeling silently enraged again.

"Now on to my final topic," Stewart continued quickly, "The FBI has dropped our investigation on your part in all this, and it won't be reopened."

Daven was eerily calm. "I had no part in this. Did you assholes even investigate Colbert at all, or was that too much to ask?"

Stewart stiffened. "Furthermore, you are expressly forbidden from retaliating against the Urbanes or the FBI in any manner whatsoever. Retaliation means a lot of things, including the refusal to be civil in official communications." He shifted his glance to the paper Daven was still holding. "You may keep a copy of the confidentiality agreement for your records, and show it to Rupert and Taylor if needed. No one else is permitted to see it."

Daven turned around to the copier and made 2 copies, then handed the original back while the fury in his heart converted rapidly to black despair.

Stewart looked down again at the recorder. "I know that your next question will be regarding Hank's sentence. I can't tell you that either, but it's in his letter. You'll know on June 15."

Daven leaned over to the device and spoke directly into it. "This is bullshit. You should all be ashamed of yourselves for letting an innocent man and his sons get separated for twenty years."

"Noted, thank you," Stewart replied dryly, a bit shocked at the outburst. "Make sure to memorize the terms of that agreement, because even one slip-up will send you to jail."

"So the boys are no longer in Los Angeles?"

"Well, yes. They're on the plane, waiting for me. We're taking them to their father first, of course, so he can say goodbye. His sentence begins tomorrow at noon."

"I refuse to believe Hank actually agreed to any of this," Daven muttered stubbornly.

Stewart shrugged. "I don't blame you for that, to be perfectly honest. But his letter should help ease your concerns."

Daven scoffed. "Well, then. I would suggest you hurry up and join the boys on that plane. The faster, the better."

Stewart cocked an eyebrow at him, but didn't react otherwise to the rude dismissal. "Goodbye, Mr. Johansson. We will be in touch."

He reached over to shake Daven's hand silently. Daven took it for some reason, he didn't know why. He secretly preferred to strangle Stewart. But the man quickly transferred a small, folded square of paper to his hand during the gesture, then left. Daven stood there dumbfounded, watching the security cameras until the three black cars disappeared out the front gate. Then he sat down hard and yanked open the piece of paper, accidentally tearing it in half from haste.

I believe Hank's claim that he was framed. We will talk more on June 15 when you come to get the letter. In the meantime, if you quit, or piss off PH and get yourself fired (or worse), I won't get approval to investigate Colbert's possible hand in all this. Be patient. I need time to think and plan how to proceed. Your silence and perfect obedience to me from now on is critical.

Daven numbly read it a few times, then went upstairs and sat down on Floyd's bed, absently scratching the bellies of the boy's two dogs as he pondered the note. "PH" meant President Hendrickson, and it would take very little to piss the man off. He and Daven actively disliked each other from their first meeting, and had never bothered to make any effort to get along. Hank was always hopeful the two men would finally click whenever an occasion put them in the same room; even trying to seat them next to each other every year at the White House's Reunited Day Dinner. He had finally talked the butler into it last year, but then Daven had deftly swapped his nameplace card with someone else's mere seconds before everyone sat down. Daven smiled at the memory of his little trick. Hank hadn't even been mad; he was too busy being impressed by his friend's ninja-like stealth and determination.

Starsky and Hutch soon fell sound asleep upside-down, and Daven reached down between his legs to massage Shannon's neck for a while. He didn't know what to do next, and was still feeling nothing over the loss of Hank's freedom. Or that of Floyd and Theo's. But he knew himself well; his tendency towards delayed reactions never meant lesser reaction. This apathy was merely the calm before the storm. The guilt, regret, and million questions would rush into his psyche all at once, and he was on the verge of being extremely miserable for at least a week.

When the intercom rang to announce dinner, it broke him out of his reverie at last. He peeled the dogs off his lap, hungrily ate the meal Chef had prepared for him, and asked Vance to drive him to church afterwards. He wanted to pray for Hank, and the boys, and even for Stewart. Especially for Stewart, maybe, he mused as he sat down in a pew and closed his eyes.

That was the plan, anyway. But the dam broke early and hard, and he ended up praying mostly for himself.

CHAPTER NINE

Friday night, March 31

Philadelphia

In a way, the last ten days had been the happiest of the Bancroft boys' lives. Their father may be all the way across the country, but he was acting how the boys thought all dads acted - meaning, not like a dictator. That's how he was on the boat every time they went sailing, and the boys loved it.

They'd all talked on the phone for hours. The man had a terrific sense of humor, who knew?

But now they were all in Philadelphia again, and Floyd in particular was dreading the possibility that the new warmth and love they'd heard over the phone would evaporate in person.

"Hey kiddo."

"Hey dad!" Theo called happily as he rushed out of the town car and into his father's arms.

"I've missed you. So glad you're here. Get any sleep on the plane?"

"No. Floyd slept the entire way, though."

"That figures. Come on, let's go to the room. What's taking him so long to get out of the car?"

Theo shrugged. "He's probably asleep again."

Hank released his youngest, then went to the car and stuck his head in.

"Hey Floyd. Put the Game Boy down and come out."

"I don't want to."

Hank clambered into the car and motioned Theo to wait with the driver.

"I know you're mad at me, but don't be a brat. There's only-"

"I'm not a brat," Floyd protested sullenly.

Hank reached over and took the gaming device gently out of the boy's hands. "I'm really glad to see you. You know we only have 14 hours. I explained this on the phone. Let's not spoil it."

"I don't want to."

"I know, because you don't want to say goodbye. Neither do I. But that's not until tomorrow. So let's go get some room service and watch TV for a bit."

"Why did Avery quit?" Floyd blurted abruptly, and Hank's heart stopped beating for a moment.

"Because he thought he wouldn't be needed anymore and got his feelings hurt when I asked him to join Daven's team."

"You didn't fight, did you?"

"Of course we did. I was really mad he wanted to leave, and I got my feelings hurt, too. There was some yelling. But leaving is what he wanted, so I wished him the best and said goodbye. Don't let that change your opinion of him. He's a really good man and deserves to be happy."

To Hank's great relief, Floyd accepted that explanation readily. "Oh. Okay."

"Let's go upstairs. I'm cold. And there's Boston cream pie on the room service menu."

That was enough to convince Floyd, and Hank climbed out after him with a grin.

At 3am, Floyd woke up with a gasping, violent start. His dad quickly came over to the bed and sat down next to him, speaking in a soothing tone and putting a warm hand on his shoulder.

"Floyd, you're with me in the hotel in Philadelphia. You okay? Sit up for a minute."

"You're awake, dad?"

"Yeah. Sit up. What were you dreaming about?"

Floyd searched his mind. "I was dreaming...something about Daven, I don't remember."

"Hmm. Anything to do with why you're being so mean to him?"

"Mean? You'd be proud, dad. I've never been more polite to anyone in my life."

"That's not what Theo says. Go back to sleep and we'll talk again in the morning."

Floyd laid back down. *Shit. So much for the new warm and fuzzy Hank Bancroft.*

It was 7am and Floyd was slowly shoveling sausages into his mouth while Theo slept on the other bed, drooling all over the bedspread. Their dad was sitting on the desk chair, absently rubbing Floyd's neck and back as he talked.

"You can't misdirect your anger like this. He didn't do anything, and doesn't deserve the way you're treating him."

Floyd bit his lip. He hadn't yet admitted what he heard on the news, about Daven being responsible for all this. His dad would certainly be furious, there was no doubt; maybe he'd even ask Daven to punish him. So Floyd had said nothing over the past week. He spent his time carefully avoiding Daven altogether, only responding to him with exceedingly polite *yes, sirs* and *no, sirs,* and not letting the man get within three feet of him or offer any comfort whatsoever.

"Floyd?" prompted Hank. "What's gotten into you? Did he do something to upset you?"

"Yeah. He doesn't have any feelings, dad. He's a robot. Maybe that's why Avery left."

Hank actually laughed out loud, and Floyd looked at him sideways. "Why is that funny?"

"Oh, if you only knew, Floyd. He's quite the character, isn't he? Look, I...there's something I really need to tell you before Theo wakes up. Are you done eating?"

"Yeah."

“Okay, put the plate down and let’s go into the living room.”

Floyd got up and stretched, feeling like he had just swallowed a brick. There were only five hours left until his dad was going to leave them for a year, and his stomach churned again as if he had eaten live snakes.

“Sit down, kiddo. This is, uh…” He put a hand on Floyd’s knee and stayed silent for a few long moments. Floyd felt his adrenalin suddenly course through his body like a racecar on the track.

“What, dad? You’re scaring me.”

Hank looked up, and his eyes were a little wet. “I don’t want you to live with Daven just yet. He’s going to be way too busy as the new leader of the Seditionists, and won’t have enough time to raise you the way I want. I’ve decided to send you to a boarding school in Virginia.”

Floyd’s expression was blank. “Just…just me?”

“You and Theo,” Hank amended. “You’ll stay there for a full year and no one will know where you are. You’ll never have to worry about the Seditionists, or photographers, or news people trying to invade our lawn, or anything like that. It’s a very safe environment.”

“Okay,” Floyd answered, not really upset about the news yet.

“The thing is, Floyd…you’re going today.”

“Today?” Floyd exclaimed.

"Today," Hank repeated. "I'm going to jail at noon, as you know, and at that time you'll be driven down to Richmond. It's about four hours. It's a training school, actually."

"For what?"

This was the hardest part of all, and Hank wasn't even sure he could ever get the words out.

"It's...just remember you're there for your own safety and security, and you'll be with Theo."

Now Floyd was really alarmed. "A training school for what?" he repeated loudly.

"For house servants. You and Theo both have-"

"We've been *indentured* ?" Floyd shouted.

Hank stood up now, too. "Yes, but only temp-Floyd, calm down and let me talk."

"Dad!"

"Floyd, *quiet*. Stop shouting. There's no reason to panic. I need to tell you all the details of what my-"

Floyd ran back into the bedroom, grabbed his coat, and slipped out the door. He took the emergency exit stairs and bolted into the lobby and out into the street. Hank and his guard didn't catch him in time.

Five hours later, the FBI came to collect their prisoner. Floyd hadn't been found yet.

They took Hank anyway.

THREE DAYS LATER

Seditionists HQ, Los Angeles

Monday morning, April 3

"Dav?" called Rupert nervously as he knocked on his boss's door. "Got a minute?"

Daven shut his laptop and pulled himself back to the present. "Yes. Come in."

Rupert visibly nervous and subdued. "You skipped church yesterday. The media is having a field day with it. Hailey, in particular. She's practically glowing."

"I don't care."

"You should, because Hank's going to kill you when he finds out."

"He won't find out," Daven answered coldly, and Rupert looked like a deer caught in the headlights as he sat down and crossed his legs one way, then the other, then back again.

"Alright. Well, Millie just called me. The boys haven't shown up for home school yet, and none of the guards are answering the phone at the house."

Daven said nothing and reached aside to grab his "World's Okayest Co-Worker" mug. The tea scorched the roof of his mouth painfully, but he didn't flinch. *Let it burn,* he thought miserably. I deserve it.

Rupert watched him closely, knowing he had to tread very lightly if he was going to get out of this conversation unscathed. "Wow. Finally using the mug I got you like six years ago, huh? I don't know if I'm more surprised by that, or by the fact that you're drinking tea."

Daven turned the cup around so the design was facing away again. "More like world's worst," he grumbled. *Uh-oh* , thought Rupert. Daven beating up on himself was rare, but always a very bad sign.

"Oh...so....Hank went down, didn't he?" Rupert asked quietly. Daven got up to lock the door, then stared out the window, not wanting to look at his friend's face for fear of starting a new grief cycle all over again. He steeled himself and spoke normally.

"Hank pled guilty and was taken to prison. The boys are now indentured and were removed from the house on Friday."

Rupert was stunned. "Excuse me? The boys were supposed to go to you. That's why they rushed this trial in the first place. What the fuck happened?"

"I don't know anything except that it was his choice. He wrote me a letter which I'll receive on June 15. I'm hoping he can explain himself then. Maybe we'll speak on the phone, eventually. For now, I..."

...I don't want to talk to him ever again. Daven mentally pushed back the nearly overwhelming fury he felt towards Hank for the incomprehensible decision. He wished he could see him one more time, just to throttle him into confetti.

Rupert said nothing for a long time. Daven heard some sniffles, so he turned to hand over some Kleenex and waited some more.

"Alright," Rupe finally said. "So what now?"

"Stewart had me sign a confidentiality agreement. I want you to sign it, too." He went to sit down, took the paper out of his pocket, and read it out loud.

"Permanent silence?" Rupe shot back angrily. "I'd have thought you would rather quit than agree to those terms."

"I may dislike the president, but he's smart enough to realize that without this agreement, our parties will spend months tearing each other apart instead of doing our jobs. I only wish he would have some the same for Hank so that he could never have instigated the problems we still have with Harmon. It's a smart move."

Rupert was shaking his head. "Dav...I don't feel the same. I can't agree to this. Ask me for my resignation if you have to."

Daven handed his colleague a pen. "You're not quitting. You're going to stay and help me get this organization back on its-"

"Dav, why would you-"

"- *back on its* feet again. That's going to take both of us. We'll still have say in what the FBI releases. We just can't release it ourselves. Tell me how that's unreasonable. Don't you dare threaten to quit on me again. You hear me?"

Rupert looked up, startled into awed silence.

"Sign it," Daven repeated firmly, before there was time for another protest. Daven's expression was unreadable, but his voice was like a thundercloud of hell about to break loose. Rupe had never heard that tone of voice before, and it shook him. So he took the pen and signed, vowing to bring the subject up again later when he might not lose his closest friend over it.

"Now," continued Daven in his normal tone, "first things first. We need to get our accounting staff back into the office. The books are going to be a mess if we don't. Can you facilitate that for me?"

"That's...it's more of a Human Resources thing, but yes. I'll get it started."

"Good. Thank you. And then I need you to gather up the latest-"

" *Wait* , Dav. Please. For god's sake, at least give me five minutes to process this clusterfuck before you throw me back into the fray."

Dav set down his mug and frowned. "Sorry. I've had three days to think about it and all I want to do now is talk about something else."

"Understood. Just bear with me a little longer. You *know* Hank was framed, right? Can't we do something?"

Daven thought again about the papers he'd been shocked to find in Hank's safe on Saturday. That was something he could tell his friend about, and it might help him move on.

"Stewart said we can't. It's done. There's something else I have to tell you. You're not going to like it."

Rupe looked crushed. "Oh, god…what? I'm afraid to know."

"Well, you need to hear it. I found out on my own that Hank's informants were making photocopies of proprietary Urbane documents for him. At least one, anyway, but it was a big one. I found it in his safe. That would explain why he always refused to tell us who his contacts were."

"Holy shit. What was it?"

"A first draft of the lawsuit Harmon filed against him. In Harmon's own handwriting, along with all his side notes and remarks."

The hair on the back of Rupert's neck rose and practically crackled from tension and fear. "Oh, fuck…Dav…that's political espionage, plain and simple."

"Yes. There's zero chance it was planted, because Hank put his own notes all over it, too."

Rupe breathed in deeply and felt like crying again. "Jesus, I've never felt so torn in my life. Who knows what else they took. Do you still have it?"

"Yes. I want to hold on for it a little bit, in case Hank appeals."

"Appeals his own guilty plea? For god's sake, Dav, you're not thinking. Get rid of it now before the FBI finds it. Nothing it says is going to help him now, if it didn't already."

"But if Stewart knew about it, he would have told me to open the safe while he was standing five feet away from it. He didn't, so he doesn't know."

Rupert went pale and clammy. "What if they show up with a search warrant? Jesus Christ on a pogo stick. How can you be so calm? You know what, it's not even safe to be telling me this. You...you *really* shouldn't have told me that."

Daven shrugged. "Like I said, I thought the knowledge that he was guilty of at least some of the charges would help you move on. It has for me. And I think it's important for you to know how much I trust you. Want to grab some breakfast with me?"

"No. I mean...thanks, but I need some time alone because I'm disturbed by how cavalier you're being about this. Seems like you don't even care what happened to Floyd and Theo," Rupert accused, even knowing he wasn't being fair. Daven wasn't exactly prone to emotion even under the roughest circumstances.

"Rupert...you of all people should know what the last three days without them has been like for me. But right now I have a lot of work to do. I'm going to the cafeteria. I hope you can pull it together by the time I get back."

"Depends how long you're gone," Rupert replied with a shrug as he got up and left. He was very upset, and Daven knew he had to change tactics quickly or his friend would walk out the door and not come back.

Got to work on your people skills, Dav. Still rusty.

—————-

Philadelphia, Monday afternoon

FBI Headquarters

Stewart rubbed his eyes as he fought with a terrible case of writer's block. Not that he didn't remember everything that happened, of course, but he had difficulty articulating it properly without breaking out into a fit of righteous indignation and accusations. This was an official report for the president, and he had to stay professional.

The prisoner was taken to Mayfair Facility and the execution postponed indefinitely, approved by Salome Danby. Approximately 90 minutes later Floyd was located by municipal police in the parking lot of Oregon Diner in South Philadelphia.

The part after that was where he had re-written his account at least four times already.

Floyd was taken by police car to Mayfair Facility and met by me, whereupon he refused to get out of the car. Mr. Bancroft was informed of this predicament, and did not grant me permission to force Floyd to exit the vehicle. A phone call was proposed as an alternative, but Floyd again refused and became emotional. Salome Danby instructed me to ensure Floyd was not having a panic attack, which he said he was not.

Stewart had to get up and walk around his office for a few minutes. He hated everything and everybody for what happened next.

After approximately 30 minutes, at 2:07pm, Floyd exited the car on his own accord and requested to be taken into the facility to say goodbye to his father.

Stewart wiped his eyes.

They embraced for approximately two minutes, during which less than twenty words were exchanged. No time limit had been given; they broke apart on their own accord. Floyd left willingly and was taken back to the hotel by police to rejoin his brother.

"Fuck you Harmon, Colbert, FBI, and everyone else involved in this bullshit," Stewart said out loud. Then he put his pen to paper again, reinvigorated by a bitter energy he had never felt before.

Hank Bancroft was executed by lethal injection at 4:00pm after reciting his final words to myself, Salome Danby, and Lester Boyd (3rd party negotiator). Please find attached the transcription of this statement.

Five long pages, single-spaced. It had been a hell-raiser of an impressive speech, too, and one which could easily start a third revolution if it got into the wrong hands. The man knew how to get a message across, to say the least.

I returned back to FBI Headquarters rather than the hotel as planned, as the emotional toll of this day exhausted my ability to continue. Salome Danby proceeded to the Ritz-Carlton on my behalf. The Bancroft boys were transported to ISTMS at 6:00pm and arrived at 10:02pm.

The report wasn't perfect, and would have to be expanded a little for more clarity, but Stewart stopped there and thought about Hank's speech again. He had taken a copy for himself, and already knew that when the investigation of Colbert was over, he was going to be calling Daven and asking for a job with the Seditionists.

MONDAY EVENING

Seditionists HQ - Los Angeles

Daven walked into Rupe's office and shut the door behind him.

"Rupert...we need to talk about what happened between us this morning. I don't want to leave it until tomorrow."

"Me either. Please sit down."

"Thanks. I should have just told you it wasn't a good time to talk in the first place. I have so much going on. I still need to explain to the household, or rather, *not* explain where the boys are. It's not going to go over well, so I've been putting it off. Hank's guards are totally in the dark too and getting on my case every five minutes for updates. Avery quit last week, by the way."

"Avery *quit* ? *Avery,* of all people? Why?"

"No idea. He left Hank alone in Philadelphia and came to say goodbye to the boys while I was at work. Theo told me."

"What a dick!"

"I'm not sleeping well," Dav continued tiredly. "The dogs are anxious about the boys missing and won't eat. I'll have 11 servants to get rid of, and almost all the guards. Not to mention two huge houses to be emptied and sold, and a boat, and cars. All the while settling Hank's personal financials and running this organization in a new role I don't feel qualified for, under the threat of jail time for making one mistake by saying something I shouldn't. My nerves are totally shot. I'm almost past caring about anything but me right now."

Now Rupert was softened up, too. "Can't blame you for that. Good god. I'm sorry. By the way, you *are* qualified. There is no one else who can do this."

"Thank you for saying that. Maybe I'll believe you one day." Daven ran a hand through his hair. "I'd like you to sign a one-year contract. I'll double your pay if you do."

"Jesus, Dav!" Rupert breathed shakily. "No. Absolutely not. I don't do things just for money."

"Then what's it going to take for you to stay?"

"Who said I was leaving?" Rupe exclaimed.

Daven spread his arms out and made a vague, all-encompassing gesture to include the entire building. "Why on earth would you *want* to stay? Do you have any idea what we're in for when the press figures this out? It's just a matter of days before everyone starts bailing on me, employees and constituents alike."

Rupe was shaking his head slowly. "I don't get it. Remember what you told me this morning? You literally said *I think it's important you know how much I trust you* . And now you're all but bribing me for a contract? What happened between then and now?"

"I realized leaving is the smartest thing to do. The safest. I would if I could."

"Then why don't you?"

Dav pursed his lips. He couldn't say that Stewart told him he can't quit, but he wanted to so desperately that it physically pained him. "I want to stay and continue Hank's work."

"I don't believe you. You want to stay behind to take down Harmon and Colbert."

"That would be a nice bonus, but no. I can't touch them, at my peril."

Rupe got it now, and his heart started to hurt, too. "I see. The FBI is forcing you to stay. For how long?"

"I don't know. For longer than I want, certainly." Daven looked broken for a moment, and Rupert suddenly felt the need to do absolutely anything to help his friend feel better. They had come so far together, why not keep going a little longer?

"Alright," he agreed, forcing out a cheerful, casual tone. "If you're that determined to be stuck with me, I'll sign a contract. Draft one up, but don't change my pay. It wouldn't look right. Just buy me dinner at Yamashiro and we'll call it even."

"Yamashiro? It might cost me less to double your pay," Dav remarked humorlessly.

"Most likely, yes. I do want a certain clause included. One that says we work together as true partners. I want to know everything that's going on with this organization. Also, you have to take my advice if I think you need rest. You drive yourself too damned hard. It's not sustainable, and god knows no one else is remotely qualified to run this ten-ring circus if you work yourself to death."

Daven nodded. "Alright. Fine. Whatever." He looked irritated, like he was going to argue, but he didn't say whatever was on his mind. Instead, he reached out to shake hands. When Rupert took it, Dav then stepped forward and pulled Rupert into a tight embrace. It was brief, but significant and unprecedented.

"Hugs now too, huh?" Rupert joked as he wiped away new moisture from his eyes and stepped back. "I might have to upgrade that mug of yours. Hey, Millie is making dinner now. Want to join us?"

"No, but thank you. I'm not in the right frame of mind. We'll talk tomorrow. Go be with your family."

"Dav...I know it always makes you uncomfortable when I say it, but you *are* part of my family, and there's always a place at our table for you. When you're ready, of course."

Daven blushed a little, as usual.

"I can't. I really need to meet with the household tonight. They're a mess. It's not fair to leave them hanging any longer."

"Oh. What are you going to tell them?"

"Well, I'm letting go of all the guards except Martinez and Toby. Then I'll tell the servants that they're going to be freed. All of them are more than halfway through their terms, so now I can legally cancel the rest of their sentences."

Rupert was stunned. "Dav, there's a massive penalty for owners to do that. Eleven of them at probably a hundred thousand a piece…that's more than your house cost."

"It's not a money issue. I intend to abolish this whole system, and who better to set an example than the new leader of the Seditionists?"

"Wait, wait. With all due respect you're being completely unrealistic. Our party is *responsible* for this system. You were one of its biggest proponents! A quarter of our constituents have servants of their own."

"But only about 5% of Harmon's. Rupe, I'm not talking about abolishing it overnight. We still have three years before we can even publicly *suggest* revoking the law. I'm talking about you and I being the drivers of a steady, gradual shift towards abolition. The program started as an alternative to prison overcrowding. It's quickly on its way to becoming full-on slavery again with every new vote."

"It's what our constituents want. You are paid to represent *their* interests, not yours. And they're going to be very confused with why you're suddenly changing trains now…or worse, just claim you're doing it only for Floyd and Theo."

Daven didn't budge. "They can claim whatever they want. Deed holders are in the minority. So we'll focus on the majority."

"In theory, yes, but...I don't know if it's possible, Dav."

"Exactly. You don't know. So why not try?"

Dav sounded so much like Hank with that statement.

"But considering our biggest supporters are the wealthy with huge households, this might be the end of both our careers if we succeed."

"God, I hope so. I hate this job."

Rupert sighed and gave up. Daven's logic and persuasive skills were not quite as irresistible as Hank's, but he had learned a lot from the man over the years. "Okay, fine. Why not. Does this mean I have to get rid of my servants, too?"

Daven fixed him with *that* look. "What do you think?"

"Right. How about I allow you to tell that one to Millie yourself?"

"I will if you insist, but as her husband it seems you-"

"Dav, I was joking. Just...let me know what you decide, so I can look into the costs."

"I've already decided."

Rupert smiled a little, feeling both dread and warmth at the same time. "Why do I have the feeling you're going to be more of a hardass than Hank Bancroft ever was?"

"That would be a difficult feat, and one that I'm not interested in accomplishing."

"Can I bring back my favorite chair, then?" Rupe joked hopefully.

Daven looked at him askance. "That hideous fluffy thing? Absolutely not."

www.ingramcontent.com/pod-product-compliance
Lightning Source LLC
Chambersburg PA
CBHW060557100726
47907CB00005B/1416